FIVE MINUTES, SIR MATTHEW

FIVE MINUTES, SIR MATTHEW

by T. C. Worsley

Alan Ross *London 1969*
30 Thurloe Place SW7

First published in Great Britain 1969 by
Allan Ross Ltd.
32 Thurloe Place S.W.7.
© T. C. Worsley
SBN 900626 00 3

Printed in England by
Billing & Sons Limited
Guildford and London

To Enid Bagnold,
the loved and envied

It is more necessary even than usual to emphasise that the characters in this book are pure fiction. There are, after all, at the moment only a limited number of actual theatrical knights. But each of them is still quite capable of filling a theatre; no one of them has only one child; no one of them has publicly defended the use of marijuana; no one of them suffers from the same aberration as my Sir Matthew. Any attempt, then, to identify him with a living character will prove idle.

T. C. W.

PART
ONE

[Sir Matthew Prior, actor, in his dressing-room in a West End Theatre, with Stephen Luther, a friend of long standing]

"You always did say I was an improbable father and I suppose I am. Everything about me is improbable really. My whole life. My success! My marriage! My aberrations! But the most improbable thing of all, the thing that strikes me as quite wholly incredible, is my age. Fifty-eight today! Can I really be? I tell you, I woke up this morning feeling thoroughly depressed. Fifty-eight? I don't feel it though, do you? . . . 'You're as old as you feel.'— balls! You're as old as you are. Look at my hands! Liver spots. The skin on my knees. I noticed in the bath today. No longer firm; wrinkled, hanging. I'm going at all the edges. . . . If I don't always look fifty-eight, its because of this front piece and the discreet help of some slap. I can see it, yes, but I can't feel it, can you? Don't you still feel that anything might happen? That we could start again? Today? Tomorrow? Couldn't it still all change one day, just as it did in the miraculous days of being young? My first improbable success, and off we went, you and I, on the strength of it, to try anything and everything?

"Well, why not now? Why coast along doing the same old things as I have for fifteen years? Why? Why? Have another drink and I'll tell you why. Because I've allowed myself to be boxed in, that's why. The trappings. The knighthood, the marriage. Success. Disastrous, all of it. It's not the sagging skin and the liver spots that stamp me as fifty-eight. It's 'Sir Matthew', and a great hulking grown-up son. A perpetual reminder. Like a fading beauty trying to conceal her age, I'm confounded by him. He makes me fifty fucking eight. . . ."

"How is he, by the way?"

"Luke . . . ? Well, Luke's Luke. Irresponsible, vain, rebellious. Girls, money, punch-ups in public. You name it, he's done it. He's in another jam now. Bow Street yet! Adrian's gone round to sort it out. He'll be in to tell us the bad news presently. I don't suppose it's anything we can't get him out of. I'm not worried. I'm used to it now. But I don't pretend to understand. They're the new lot of actors, you know. Good looks, charm, youth, success; they've got the lot, and they trade on it. Thoroughly ill-disciplined, living it up, young hell-raisers. They get it so bloody easy these days. No talent. No hard work. Nothing but their looks. That's not the theatre I was brought up in. . . .

"Yes, now I'm talking like fifty-eight, I know. But he makes me. Only twenty, and everything before him and chucking it away. And its all my fault, you see. Having this beat-up *passé* star for a father, he has to rebel against the name. He uses it, and then kicks me in the teeth for giving it him. Or would if I let him. . . . But I don't. I just refuse the responsibility. I'll get him out of this mess whatever it is, if I can. But I won't feel guilty. If he likes to mess up his life, he's twenty and it's his affair. . . . In the largest view I suppose all parents are responsible for what their children become. But the largest view is just too large for me.

"No, if I'm to feel guilty at all, I'll feel guilty over Grace. But then I *am* guilty over Grace. She naturally accuses me of the responsibility for Luke's behaviour. But what she's really accusing me of is my irresponsibility over her, and I can only plead guilty to that."

"Sorry, Matt, I didn't know you had someone . . ."

"It's only old Stephen. He flew in this morning. You remember Stephen?"

"Good lord, Stephen ducky. How are you? Look, I'm sorry, but I must talk to Matt. Real disaster this time."

"What's happened?"

"If Stephen wouldn't mind . . ."

"You can say anything in front of Stephen. He and I were in trouble together before you were born."

"It's drugs now, my dear."

"Oh God, not that too."

"Yes, he was going to this party, you see. And just at the door the Law arrived. It seems that he'd done something silly with a cheque. And they came to enquire."

"Bloody little fool. I thought he was flush enough. Why didn't he come to me?"

"And then they searched him. He was carrying this parcel, and they opened it. It was hash."

"Hash?"

12

"Marijuana, cannabis, hemp, the real stuff. Quite a block of it. That's what they're holding him for—illegal possession."

"I didn't know he was on the drugs, did you?"

"Yes, I suppose I did. They all are, my dear."

"Well, get hold of Cruddle and fix it all up, can't you. I'm on in fifteen minutes."

"I've done that already, we're meeting at Bow Street at 8 o'clock—that's where he is. But I thought I'd better tell you. It'll be in the papers for sure."

"Couldn't you stop that?"

"I doubt it, but I'll try. See you after the show."

"I'm giving Stephen dinner after . . ."

"All the same. . . ."

"All right, then, come and join us and tell us the worst. How long has it been going on, this drug bit?"

"Some little time I think."

"Where the hell does he get it from?"

"From Jason Squire, I imagine."

"What, that bloody pop singer? I didn't know they were mates."

"Very close, just lately. Jason's just got back from Sweden and handed the stuff to Luke for this party. . . ."

"God damn him. Well, there we are. Get round there and fix it up, bail him out, and do what you can to keep it quiet.

"I will, don't worry."

[And Adrian left.]

14

"Worry! I should worry! Him and those bloody young performers with their intellectual pretentions and their cult of freedom. This isn't going to look very pretty, is it? 'Famous actor's son on drug charge.' Very good for my image! Damn and blast them all."

"I wish I could help somehow."

"Stay around! You help by being here. You're someone I can talk to. You always have been. . . . Yet I don't know why I should pretend to be shocked by the drugs all the same. It was just never one of our temptations, was it? But we're hardly in a position to be moral about a vice which we don't happen to share. . . . After all, it's no worse than whisky, is it? Have another. I need one after that. Anyhow, this is something he can't blame me for. Drugs are his problem, not mine. They're in the contemporary air. But they were never in ours, were they? He's got in with this crowd who live for kicks in the moment, and drugs is one of them. . . . I see in a way that's a revolt against me and my name. I stand among his lot for the oldest of old hat. Carrying my name about he has to assert that he's the newest of the new, to

be more with-it than anyone. Just to show. As
long as he doesn't go on from that to the hard
stuff. I certainly hope the poor little brute's not
on them. . . . I've never tried any of them, have
you? I've always thought of them as killers. But
whisky's a killer, too, I suppose. And I've been
drinking too much of that for years as everyone
knows. . . . Hell! . . . Do you know, I expect it's
a marvellous pleasure if one could ration oneself. Can one? I must find out.

> [*A voice over the tannoy*—
> "Fifteen minutes, Sir
> Matthew."]

"I really shouldn't bother to come if I were
you, Stephen. You've seen it all before and
properly in context. This is just a rehash of past
successes, a string of Coward, Dodie Smith, and
Thirties tat. I don't know why I'm doing it.
Parading my past in what's virtually a one-
man recital. 'PRESENTING Matthew Prior in
SCENES FROM . . . with the help of Miss A and
Miss B.' They persuaded me, Adrian and the
others, after our second flop. The others all did
one. Johnny did his Shakers, Emlyn his
Dickens. So they said why not dream me up

16

something? It's safe, I suppose. They come in droves, the old ladies, the middle-aged. It reminds them of their youth, and me, too, I guess. I'm not the success I was, you know."

"You haven't done very much in the last two years, I noticed."

"No, I'm out of fashion. They can't stand me, the new lot. Luke will tell you. They give imitations of my mannerisms . . .

[*and he imitated his own Shakespearean manner*]
'Where souls do couch on
flowers we'll hand in hand
And with our sprightly port
make the ghosts gaze.'

I can hear them doing it. I'm simply not 'in', and two crashing flops have made that clear. It's the most fashion-bound art of all of them, ours. And I'm just out. So up I get now and flute and flutter through all the old favourites for all those who are as *passé* as myself. It's shaming, really, shaming.

"Of course, the fashion will change."

"Will it? I wonder. In any case, how long can I wait? If only I'd been something else, a writer or a painter, then fashion wouldn't matter. I could go on in my own way until the tide turned, or defy the tide, come to that. But in this business you're so dependent on them out there. What can I do? Stand aside? I'd just be forgotten. . . . In three months they'd be saying: Him? I thought he was dead. No, I tell you Stephen, I'm in a bad patch. Thank God I've always been sensible over money, and lucky—lucky to have made it when you could still keep it. I'm all right there. But as far as my career goes, I ought to face it . . . it's finished. . . . But dammit, it doesn't feel finished. . . . *I* don't feel finished. I'm free-wheeling at the moment, I know. Have been for fifteen years really, waiting for something to turn up. And when it did I could start again. That's how it seemed. And that's how it still seems. Wave a wand, cancel the years and anything might happen. Anything in the world. Don't you feel the same?

[*Voice again on the tannoy—*
"Five minutes, Sir
Matthew."]

You'd better go then, if you *are* coming. It may bring back some old memories. If we can't look forward, I suppose we can always look back."

[Extract from Stephen Luther's Diary]

GOT home from Africa yesterday. For good
now. My job taken over, by one of my own old
pupils ironically enough. But it's as it should be,
and I'm so well pensioned I can have no complaints. Round to Matthew, as always, when I
got back to this country. Welcomed, as always,
as if I'd only been a week away instead of two
years. That's his special trick. When you're
away, you imagine yourself completely forgotten. Has he ever written a letter in his life?
But when you're in touch with him again, you're
drawn right in, made free of his private dramas
and thoughts, assigned your special place, your
particular rôle.

Mine is, as it always has been, the sym-
pathetic ear. Who plays this rôle when I'm not
there? Not Adrian, surely: his is a different
part. He is a client in the old classical sense. I
remember from my schooldays how that word
cliens always baffled me: the translation as
"client" representing a quite different relationship, that between yourself and, say, solicitors

19

or stockbrokers. But I should have understood the word if I had met an Adrian in those days, a combination of factotum and yes-man. A paid flatterer, to be really bitchy. Matthew has always had one or more of those around him. Very bad for him, too. They may boost his morale, but they also encourage the worst in him, his failure to recognise the truth about himself and the world he lives in.

But we mustn't underestimate the Adrians, either. This one has a sharp tongue and a certain activity, though of a very limited kind. When I told him I was home for good he was slightly put out:

"Will you be around all the time?"

I said I wasn't sure that I'ld stay in this country. He bridled, and then remembering his duty as a client, he admitted:

"Matthew will want you to. He misses you."

I said I supposed so, rather doubtfully, having in mind that Matthew hadn't even enquired how long I was here for, how I was getting on or made any of even the most conventional attempts to appear interested in me. As I said:

"The monologue goes on. Does it go on without me?"

"What do you think, ducky?" was Adrian's retort.

"Then why should he want me especially?" I wondered.

"Different sounding boards give off different notes," Adrian rather shrewdly said. "And he particularly values yours."

Perhaps he always has revealed himself more to me than to most people. And I seemed to detect a rather more desperate note in his complaints this time. Of course the same difficulty arises for a male beauty as for a female, especially in his profession, as the years advance. And Matthew was a beauty.

"He must have been gorgeous at twenty," Adrian remarked, apropos of nostalgia growing on him.

And, of course, he was; and it's no good denying that a very considerable part of his success depended on that beauty. His use of it was his gift, of course. But there it was for him to use.

Not that he's getting old at all. It really does seem incredible that he's fifty-eight. He could still play forty with complete conviction, I should say. But it is quite true that he is in a sort of vacuum at the moment. The recital he's doing is really contemptible. Of course it's done with great "taste", of a rather camp kind: that's what his promoters are especially good at. But the stuff itself is really hardly worth preserving at any time, and certainly not in this sort of Gems from the Classics guise. It only shows up really how very far from classics those Thirties things were. It is—to be bitchy again —a real Adrian idea of a theatrical evening.

And Adrian made a very typical client's remark apropos of it. He said when I had commented that I didn't quite know how to comfort Matthew over it:

"You can tell him how marvellous it is."

"But I don't think it is."

"Then pretend, ducky. What are we here for?"

Exactly; what are they there for, the clients, except to pretend that everything in the garden is lovely? That's never been my role. Indeed, the very opposite. It was just my not being a client in that sense that first attracted him to me in the old days. He needed my dash of realism just as much as he needed their flattery.

But I'm not sure that this—my realism—is going to be much use now. I can't turn back the clock. He is fifty-eight and accepting the fact won't make it more palatable.

Certainly he shouldn't be doing a mere pot-pourri like this recital. But what should he be doing? What is there that he could do that he hasn't done? Presumably his advisers and promoters have thought of everything they can, and they certainly know more than I do about what's available. But I should have thought something better than this could have been found. I must give my mind to it.

As to the Luke imbroglio, where it specially hits Matthew, I suppose, is that it brings up all too vividly the generation question. Luke has so completely identified himself with the new *avant-garde* theatre and the new generation of actors. Why he thinks it necessary to carry his revolt to quite such a pitch is another question. If he had been a complete flop himself as an actor it would have been understandable. But on the contrary he made a very big hit, got that film contract straight from his first Royal Court play, and made a blazing success of that. Why on earth shouldn't that have satisfied him? That he's in some way hitting at Matthew over it seems an inescapable conclusion.

Matthew's reaction is very ambivalent. I

suspect that he's really rather proud of Luke underneath, though he's not going to say so while Luke is so obviously rebelling against him personally. Fond of him, too, perhaps, at heart. But it is rather hard when Luke can be said to stand for all the values—or lack of them, Matthew would say—that are driving Matthew himself into the cold. It certainly complicates the situation.

24

BRIAN HURLEY TAKES TEA WITH
MATTHEW PRIOR AT 58

AN interview with Matthew Prior is never like any other interview. Not for him the carefully arranged conversation in the carefully arranged room.

I found him on his croquet lawn in his Hampshire house practising devilish shots and making up combinations of intricate and scintillating tactics. You might think that just now he would be disturbed or worried. But not if you knew Matthew Prior.

He didn't seem in the least disturbed by the family ructions which have broken out in his usually placid family life.

"You know what the young are," he said judiciously. "Haven't we all got into these pickles in our youth? It's all been grossly exaggerated, anyhow. If Luke had had a different name, nothing would have been heard of it. It's the price one pays for this absurd celebrity nonsense."

And he refused to talk about that subject any more. "Let's talk about something more interesting," he said, leading me in through the french windows to where tea was laid out in the airy drawing-room. Cucumber sandwiches and the thinnest of thin bread and butter. Delicate China tea. The walls are crowded with pictures. Modern but not aggressively so.

"Pop art," he said, when I mentioned them," is the new movement I *can* do with. That's a

25

David Hockney. I got it the other day. Do you like it?"

I murmured appreciation, and asked him if there was any corresponding movement in the theatre that he went for.

"Too much is made of movements," he said reflectively. "It helps the critics, I suppose, to group things together. I admire individuals, not movements."

"Which individuals?" I probed.

But he refused to be drawn. "If I mention one and not another, you'll assume I dislike the ones I don't mention, and dog doesn't eat dog."

"But do you find a great change in the theatre from the theatre of your day?"

"I don't know that my day is over yet," he said, with a trace of acerbity. "But of course there's a change, yes. Nothing stands still. I find the theatre in a very healthy state of unrest. That's as it should be, and the exciting thing is that the young are now interested in it once again. In what you are pleased to call 'my day', the young were interested only in the novel or films. Now when a young man starts writing, he may as easily turn to the play form as any other. That's very healthy."

"You don't appear in their plays, though, do you?" I asked.

"If one were written for me, I certainly would," he said. "But I'm rather a special kind of actor," he admitted. "I don't fit easily into this new movement."

"Do you regret that?" I asked him.

"It's not much good regretting what can't be changed," he said, with another touch of acerbity. "Besides, it won't last for ever, you know; fashions change."

"And you think your kind of acting will have a come-back?"

"I don't know about a come-back. You talk as if I'm finished. Don't make that mistake.'

26

"You had your fifty-eighth birthday last week," I reminded him. "How do you feel about that?"

"How should I feel about it?" he said belligerently. "I don't feel old, if that's what you mean."

He didn't look old either, in his pink shirt and blue slacks. He lookd as slim and vigorous as ever.

I came away feeling pretty certain that we shall be seeing Matthew Prior up there again pretty soon in something more substantial than "Scenes from . . .". There was a certain aggressiveness about him that augurs ill for those who think he is finished.

Beneath his county suavity, there is a fighter waiting to get out.

[*Letter from Luke Prior*]

DARLING JOANIE,

Thank you for your kind thoughts for me "in my troubles" as you put it. And, as you say, being Matthew Prior's son has distinctly not helped. There'd have been none of this fuss otherwise. Shit to it all. But I wish he wouldn't be so bloody condescending. Did you see that interview he gave yesterday to Brian Hurley —wouldn't it be more decent to keep quiet in the circumstances? He said: Haven't we all got into pickles in our youth? "Pickles", for Christ's sake. And there was another bit about our "placid family circle". From Brian Hurley, I ask you, who knows all the dirt down to the last particle. And why, for God's sake, does he have to go on courting the young, as if they give a fuck whether he approves of them or not? But he simply can't resist it.

That's why I can't face him. I could face *this* all right, but I really can't put up with all that pompous Sir Matthew stuff.

It was real bad luck, you know; that's what

makes it worse. I was just going out to a party with this stuff Jason had given me for it, when the fuzz arrived. I was having some trouble about a cheque, and that's what they'd really come for. And I had tried this stuff and they smelt it, and there we were—in Bow Street.

I panicked a bit and got on to Adrian, and he whisked Cruddle the solicitor round and they bailed me out. And I'm on remand for a week. Now, of course, they're on to me, badgering me to attend conferences and God knows what. Engaging grand counsel and all that. You see why, of course; it isn't me they're interested in, it's the name they're trying to protect. If it was just me I'd ride it through. What's six months in gaol, anyhow? Chalk it up to experience. But not being me, being just an appendage, I've got to grovel and plead ignorance and all that cock. But I'm not going to any more of their conferences, I can tell them that. I'm not giving them the satisfaction of seeing me grovelling and having me saying Yes sir, and No, sir. And being lectured by him on all he's done for me. Not on your nelly I'm not.

Why on earth didn't I take a different name when I started out? It would have saved all this. Then I'd never have had to be mixed up with the Matthew Prior circus any longer. It just shows how innocent I was in those days! Mug Luke really believing, actually *believing*, that he was a great success and we were a happy family. Fuck innocence.

Oh God, all about me as usual! But you do see it's bloody, don't you? See you at the weekend. Same time as usual, and Sunday we'll drive out somewhere and forget it all.

Your very loving

LUKE

*[Interview between Sir Matthew and his
Solicitor, Alfred Cruddle]*

"IT's very good of you to have come round,
Cruddle. But there's no sign of Master Luke
yet, I'm afraid."

"Doesn't he want to defend himself?"

"Not particularly, I imagine. At the moment,
anyhow, I suspect he's quite content with the
damage he's done, and isn't the least anxious
to undo it yet."

"Six months inside would cool him off."

"I wonder. The disgrace of prison is a thing
of the past, you know. No one thinks any the
worse of the young for doing a stretch. On the
contrary, it's quite chic. All the best people
from Arnold Wesker downwards have done
their spell. No, I dare say he'd like a stretch
to boast about. But, of course, he'd like it
more if it could be made to seem that
his father had cruelly abandoned him to his
fate. So we must counter that by doing
everything we can to save him from himself,
as they say."

31

"There's not much we can do, if he won't co-operate at all."

"You'll think of something. You always do. Besides, when it comes to the point, you'll find he turns up sulkily and submits. Otherwise he'll look a fool, and he won't want that. But he'll make us suffer as long as he can."

"You seem to know him pretty well."

"Do I, indeed? Well, in fact, I don't think I know him at all, not at all. This father business is an impossible relationship. Do you know *your* children? What, a girl and a boy, isn't it?"

"Well, they're pretty straightforward, you know. The girl's engaged to a nice young fellow. The boy will come into the firm."

"So you think you've been a pretty good father?"

"I don't think about it, to tell you the truth."

"Of course. That's exactly how the relationship should be, if it's to work. You don't think about it; they don't think about it; it's simply accepted for what it is. It's when either side does start thinking that the trouble begins. . . . No, I don't *know* Luke at all. But I know what it is to be young and damaged."

"As an actor, of course, you have to put yourself in other people's shoes."

"No, that's bunk, too. I know it as a particular sort of man. How old are you, Cruddle?"

"Since you ask, fifty-six."

"Do you feel fifty-six?"

"My rheumatism ensures I do! And my position and my children, yes. Yes, I feel fifty-six. It's not so old as all that, you know. I've got a few good years left, and then I dare say I shall be glad to hand over when the time comes. And Clem—that's the son—will be there to take on."

"How beautifully simple! Don't you feel jealous, envious? Don't you, at times, wish them—out of the way?"

"Who?"

"Why, the young, the hungry generations, hungry to tread us down."

"What an odd fellow you are, Prior. What an extraordinary way to look at it!"

"It's not really, you know. It's quite usual. You feel it too, or would if you let yourself."

"Now, about young Luke . . ."

"Yes, young Luke. He was a sweet boy as a child, loving and devoted. I expect I took it too much for granted. I feed on admiration, you know. I expect it. I exact it. And I don't give much in return. I expect that's the trouble."

"Nonsense. You've given him too much. You've spoiled him."

"I've given what cost me nothing to give, which isn't giving really. It's buying."

"You've given him as good a start in life as any young man could want. And he seemed to be doing so well. The young get it too easy nowadays."

"Now come off it, when we find ourselves talking like this we ought to take a pull on ourselves. We're betraying nothing but our age. It's as difficult to be young as ever it was."

"I won't subscribe to that. Luke had it easy with your name behind him and no worries about money."

"But one still has to find oneself, to reach down to the essential *me*, to disentangle that essential *me* from all the accretions, hereditary and social, that have gathered round the possibility of *me*, the potentiality of *me*; and the more heavily charged those accretions are, the more difficult it is to fight one's way out of them."

"You're talking above my head, and muddling yourself to find excuses for the inexcusable. Luke's behaviour is inexcusable."

"Yes, I'll give you that. Let's treat him as inexcusable, but rescue him if we can."

34

"If we go about it the right way, he'll get off with a heavy fine and probation. How will he respond to probation?"

"Appallingly, I suppose."

"Well, what's to be done about him?"

"He must work things out for himself. We can't work them out for him. We can only stand by to pick up the pieces. And the pieces will probably be pieces of us, not him."

"That's just what I'm worried about. If the lad likes to make a complete mess of his life, that's his affair, as I shall tell him. But it's all so bad for you and Grace."

"As for Grace, it gives her a big chance to practise her amateur psychology on us all. And as for me, it won't do me any harm."

"But it will, you know. The public doesn't like this sort of thing. And they don't remember details. If mud is flung around, it sticks, and some of it will inevitably stick to you."

"As far as that goes the public—if there is such a thing—have already, what shall I say, faltered in their allegiance. I'm no longer what I was."

"I wouldn't say that."

"My accountant does, and he's the modern arbiter."

"What you want is a good holiday. Take one when this is all over."

"Sensible, practical Cruddle! Fifty-six and a good father, with agreeable, docile children. Take a good holiday. Pull yourself together!"

"How is Grace taking it?"

"Oh, she blames me, of course. I've neglected Luke. I'm so self-absorbed that I don't see what's going on under my nose. I'm an ego-centric monomaniac and I drink too much."

"That's not very helpful."

"No, but it's true."

"I suppose an actor has to be rather self-absorbed."

"But a father shouldn't be, even an improbable father like me. That's what my old friend Stephen Luther called me. An improbable father! Do I strike you as that, Cruddle?"

"I can't think what the fellow meant. How can one be an improbable father. You artistic fellows defeat me sometimes."

"And you practical fellows are such a comfort to us. You deal with the realities we evade on our behalf. Thank goodness for you. Will you deal with my squalid realities for me, if they catch up with me, Cruddle?"

"Now what are you talking about?"

"Tell me, Cruddle, how do I strike you, objectively? What am I in your eyes?"

"A thoroughly successful actor going through a bad patch through the follies of a delinquent son."

"And up till then?"

"How do you mean?"

"If someone in the club, say, said to you, 'that Matthew Prior's a client of yours, isn't he? What sort of chap is he?' What would you say?"

"I wouldn't discuss a client of mine with an acquaintance in a club."

"But suppose you did? Suppose you had inconceivably had one more than usual and were in a confidential mood, what would you say, what sort of chap would you say I was?"

"It's too difficult to say. It's embarrassing . . ."

"Go on, have a shot. Let yourself go for once."

"Let me think then. I should say you were a very good type. Surprisingly modest for one who was so well known. Great charm—oh dear, this is difficult. . . . Not at all what actors are supposed to be, you know, bohemian and all that. . . .

37

"A gentleman like any other, would you say?"

"Of course. A pity, I should say, that you didn't really get on with your wife and she such a charming woman. But there's nothing unusual about that."

"You don't make me sound very interesting."

"Well, if we must play this game, I think the other fellow would expect something hectic in the life of a successful actor. Revelations, if you know what I mean."

"And you wouldn't have any to give?"

"No, I wouldn't, would I?"

"Just a family man?"

"Not exactly that, no. But nearer than he would think. Look here, let's drop this. I'm no good at these sort of fancies."

"Meanwhile, as I prophesied, Luke remains missing."

"Have you thought of trying a psychiatrist?"

"Me?"

"For him, I mean. You don't need one. Mind you, I'm not sure how much good these psychos do. But it might be worth trying one for Master Luke. Enoch Evans is a very good man. Do you know him?"

"I don't think I do."

"I thought you might have come across him. He belongs to the Garrick. I'll give you an introduction if you like."

"It might be worth trying, if we ever get to the point where Luke and I talk again. Meanwhile I'm sorry to have wasted your time."

"It hasn't been wasted. I've enjoyed our chat. Don't worry too much. We'll do something."

"I know you will. I rely on you to. Do I have to do anything?"

"We'll be putting you in the box, of course."

"I suppose that can't be avoided?"

"No, you've got to do your line about guaranteeing his overdraft. Besides, the magistrate—old Robertson, if it is old Robertson—will be impressed having you there."

"Nothing else?"

"It's possible the police may want to come and talk to you."

"What do I say then?"

"As little as possible. But you'll find they'll want to help more than anything. They won't be vindictive about it. They're worried about the drug traffic side of it, and naturally want all the help they can get to clamp down on that."

"I suppose that *is* natural."

39

"Of course. We don't want an American-sized problem on our hands here, do we?"

"I've never taken them, have you?"

"Good heavens, no."

"Wouldn't you rather like to try?"

"I would not. Nor would you, if you had any sense. You need that holiday, Prior. Badly. We'll get this all straightened out next week, and then take yourself off somewhere. Meanwhile keep your pecker up."

"What extraordinary expressions you use so innocently, Cruddle."

"What do you mean?"

"Oh, nothing, Keep in touch."

"You'll be hearing from me. I'll aim at the day after tomorrow."

our responsibility — we've done it, so badly.

[Letter from Grace Prior]

DEAR MATTHEW,

Isn't this appalling about Luke? What
can we do to rescue him from this dreadful
habit? I think you should try and see whether
you can't persuade him to go to a good
psychiatrist. I have the names of several who
specialise in this kind of thing and I will find
out who is considered the very best, and let you
know. And then you must get in touch with
him and *make* him go.

But I don't think even that is enough. I was
awake *all* last night thinking about it and this
was the conclusion I came to. Luke was a baby,
you must remember, when the first difficulties
arose in our marriage, and all those vulnerable
years were spent in an atmosphere of *dissension*.
It's to that that I attribute his disturbed state
now. That's what *we've* done to him. Yes, I'm
taking my share of the blame, too. But what I
say now is that at least we might make an
effort now for his sake. It's *our* responsibility.
Supposing he saw us *happily* together now, don't

you think it might make a great difference?

After all, Matthew, you're now fifty-eight. Don't you think at this age it's time *you* faced *your* responsibilities? We don't get on so badly. I know you're in a bad patch at the moment, and those beastly critics won't leave you alone (did you see that horrible piece from that little skunk, Hobson, in the Sunday Supplement?). But don't imagine it will always be like this. Your *wonderful* gifts are not going to be wasted. They can't be. They mustn't be. And I think I could help over that. You know if you'd shown me those two last plays, I should *never* have let you do them. We must search very carefully and find *just the right thing*, and it will be all right again. Wasn't I a real help in picking and choosing in the old days? I have ideas still. I don't think your present friends are good advisers.

Think it over carefully, Matthew dear, and I think you'll see that it wouldn't be only to Luke's advantage if we settled down together now: it would be to your own too. And I'm sure if we tried we could make a go of it. Think it over and let me know.

Affectionately,
GRACE

"WHAT appals me, you see, is that people like Cruddle think I've joined them. Just because I'm called 'Sir'. They count me as one of them. But I've not become a Cruddle, for God's sake, have I? I don't subscribe to any of it. To their boring moral clichés, their dead distinctions, their ghastly playing safe, their blocking all progress when it's good, and turning the blind eye when it's absolutely disastrous. The Establishment. The people who've got us into our present mess—lawyers, administrators, tycoons, soldiers, legislators. The doers who've stopped even doing now, who are quite happy provided the daughter marries well, and the boy comes into the firm, while the heavens are falling about them.

"But what am I, then, if I'm not one of them? An artist. And a bloody good one. Or was; or was. . . . A talent and nothing but a talent. . . . For, you see, I don't subscribe either to the fashionable view that artists are superior beings who change the world. They're just people with

43

special talents, at the disposal of the community. Those men of action, they're the people who ought to be making a civilisation when all they're making is a muck-heap. And when they'd done it they'ld call us in to add a spice to life. That's all the arts are, just a spice to life when you can afford them. They don't affect it. Otherwise all our arty friends would be much better than anyone else, but I haven't noticed they are, have you? . . .

"No, the past knew much better how to treat its artists: 'I want that ceiling decorated with an Aphrodité motif. Get on with it.' 'We've got a state marriage coming up in a couple of months. We shall want a romantic comedy, and it had better include a wedding scene.'

"Now, God dammit, it's Yes, Sir Matthew, Marvellous, Sir Matthew. How do you do it, Sir Matthew? No, you know there's more to be said for Luke and his lot than I've allowed for. They've avoided the trap. They don't give a fuck, so they don't have to worry. No position, so nothing to lose. Not like me, stuck up here on top of a knighthood. And it's my own silly fault. Building up this façade and trying to live up to it.

"How much happier we were, when we

44

cared for nobody in those far off university days. Forty years ago, almost. Do you remember? Goodness, how clearly I remember you. You were absurd, dear Stephen. So difficult, so edgy, so on the defensive, in your ridiculous baggy suits, thinking beer grown up, and life meant for work. You didn't know how to play. You held me off for, how long was it? A term and a half? Longer than anyone ever had. You knew nothing about life, nothing about yourself, you didn't know how handsome you were, and you were terrified—terrified of discovering you might like it all too much. You used to sit looking down your pretty nose at me, despising my frivolity, lecturing me on being 'serious', insisting that I read, and ordering me what to read. I adored it. No one had ever treated me like that.

"Your rooms were hideous. You even prided yourself on their sparseness. I had to make all the running. At first you even affected to dislike it. I was interrupting your work. Then you would grudgingly offer me a gasper and a glass of tolly. Nothing stronger ever. Your bedroom was bleak, your pyjamas flannel, your dressing-gown hairy. If you'd been young today, I should think you'ld have had a beard.

"Well, I persisted and won. Gradually, grudgingly, fighting every inch of the way. You gave in and you found you liked it. And then those five marvellous years. You ought never to have left me. Oh, I know you had that offer, somewhere in the colonies, wasn't it? And you had to accept it. But you were my talisman and my conscience. You had a stronger sense of reality. You'd never have let me take the next false steps. What *was* the temptation, I wonder now, to the middle-class trappings, the marriage, the country house, the Albany flat, the posh gentlemanly life? Or is it just that, like children, we want it all ways? Social acceptance on the one hand, but the right to do what we like on the other. That's the trap."

"Still, you've got away with it. . . ."

"Miraculously, haven't I? So far, anyhow. But you see the fact is, this business of Luke's is upsetting me not because of him but because of me. And I don't mean it the way dear old Cruddle imagined. Dirt flung, dirt sticking. I mean all the police business and lawyers. It sends shivers down my spine. I hate it. I loathe it. It brings the nagging anxiety back. It's as if not Luke but I had been caught out. As if they'll turn any day and point the finger at me.

46

I tell you, I have the greatest difficulty in not giving the game away with someone like Cruddle. Something in me longs to say 'Oh come off it! Don't you know what I'm really like?' I suppose it's the need for punishment the guilty all feel.

"But when this is all over, when we've got Luke out of this mess, I've a good mind just to give in. What a relief that would be! And I've nothing to lose. Grace and I hardly ever speak to each other except in company. By a tacit agreement we alternate in the country and in London. I don't care any longer, do I, about the façade? Why keep it up? Why not duck out? I can afford it. Why not stop pretending? It isn't as if anyone gives a fart any longer whether I appear in another play or not. It would save them embarrassment if I didn't. As for this nonsense I'm doing now, I tell you I can hardly bear to go on with it one day longer. We were taking it to America. Well, that's off, I can tell them now. And I shan't keep it up much longer here. One day, if this goes on, I shall just go out there and say: fuck off all of you, and take your money with you. This is a shaming sham, and you ought to know it. . . ."

"And then?"

"Yes, yes. What then? It's not as if I can do anything else but act. It's all I'm born for. I can't write or paint. I can't just do nothing. A new start, I think, you see. A fresh clean slate. But a new start at what? It's all a delusion, isn't it? There's no new start at fifty-eight, is there? How can one change at this stage? Yes, I see, I see. It's somewhere round here that the fatal flaw in our way of life is buried, the delusion that we're as young as we feel, and that there's still any amount of time; time to change, time to be quite different. But there isn't. Time's running out fast. We are what we have become. Yes, that's the sad and rueful truth we kind of people can't and won't face—we are what we've become. . . ."

48

[Sir Matthew and Adrian Summers in the Albany flat]

"DID you see Grace's letter?"

"Yes, I had a peep. She is the bitch, isn't she?"

"No, she isn't. She's just a sweet, silly woman who's got on to Freud and Adler late in life. And what she's suggesting is what they all suggest. Back to domestic respectability, and then everyone approves of you."

"But get her talking about her ideas for plays! There she goes too far, she really does. Who thought of that grisly one about Tiberius, I should like to know! She doesn't claim credit for that, I notice!"

"Not that we seem to have been exactly successful for ourselves with our last two efforts."

"Now, you know what the trouble there was. It was nothing to do with you. It was simply bad casting all round. We let Angy have far too much his own way. It's him who's out of touch, not you."

"No, don't let's fool ourselves. I'm out. Not for ever, perhaps. But for the moment. Ask the critics. They aren't going to allow me any merit at all. I'm old hat, finished. . . ."

"Oh, the critics. . . !"

"Wait a minute. I'm not being self-pitying about it. I had a long run. I was their darling for twenty years. I can't complain now if they want something different. My particular gifts, if I've got any, can't find a place in this new raucous, regional theatre. Don't think I'm running it down. I quite see its vitality and I quite see I don't fit into it. The Liverpool sound and the *voix d'argent* don't mix, and if it has a style of its own, it's not my style. We must face all that. The thing is what the hell am I to do next. Because I can tell you I'm not going on with this much longer."

"There's always Spiegel's offer and George Cukor's. You can make a lot of money in Hollywood still."

"I wasn't thinking of the money. Yes, I can always fit into the Bible or the Roman epics somewhere. They think it distinguished to have someone like me playing a minor prophet or a Roman judge. But that's hardly getting me anywhere, is it?"

"I think we ought to do a lovely revival."

"Of what?"

"What about one of Wilde's; they always go down well."

"All tarted up by Cecil Beaton? No, for God's sake, we've had that. No, I suppose we shall just have to wait until something does come along. But what? They all think I can go on playing Hamlet at fifty-eight."

"Forbes Robertson was still playing it at sixty, ducky."

"But he wasn't faced with competition from a Redbrick student with a long scarf and a Birmingham accent, which is the Prince of the modern fashion. You can't see me trying that I hope."

"No. But I'm going to talk to you very severely, my dear. You're not to get bitter. It isn't the critics that matter; it's the public, and there's a great big public that *wants* you. They're flocking in now aren't they?"

"Yes, to this hash-up of past successes. Living on the past like me. . . . What am I to say to Grace?"

"Say just what you feel, my dear, it will do her good."

"And what do I feel? Well, I suppose what I feel is that that really would be giving up. Start a cosy old Darby and Joan old age? Perhaps she's right. Perhaps I should, perhaps it's time I did. But I can't and won't. Meanwhile, have you seen Luke?"

"Yes, I have as a matter of fact."

"I thought you might have. And what does he say for himself?"

"Oh lots. How it was all your fault and, anyhow, he'd done nothing very wrong, and why didn't you all leave him alone? All you were worried about was your own image—you don't care a damn about him—and so on. Poor Luke! He feels very hard done by."

"You've always been soft about Luke."

"Well, he's so pretty, isn't he? But seriously, what are you going to do about him?"

"What can I do except provide the best advice I can and get him off as cheaply as possible. And he won't even bother to turn up for a conference."

"You ought to talk to him, my dear."

"Christ Almighty, he won't even see me. I'm not going on my knees to beg him. He knows where to find me if he wants me."

"I expect, in spite of everything, he wants to feel you care."

"Well, I don't. Not about him. He's quite right. I care about the headlines that are going to imply I'm a hopeless father. That's what I care about."

"Couldn't you write him a line?"

"Saying what?"

"You're sorry for him or something. Just put yourself out for him a little."

"God Almighty, aren't I doing that already, wasting hours of time with solicitors and barristers and all?"

"Still, make another effort."

"O.K. I'll write something. God knows what. Hang on for a bit. You can take it round to him. . . . Have you ever tried this marijuana?"

"Several times."

"What's it like?"

"It affects different people different ways. For me, it makes it last longer, if you know what I mean."

"Where do you get it from?"

"There's a pub in the Tottenham Court Road. You can always get a few cigarettes there, if that's all you want."

"I'd rather like to try it."

"Nothing simpler. I'll get you some."

"Any old time. . . . I don't know what I can say to the boy that he'll listen to anyway. . . . Oh well, I'll go and have a try."

[*From Stephen Luther's Diary*]

LIVING abroad, one doesn't properly realise how completely England has changed in the last ten years. The whole scene really is different. And I think it's more than just superficial, as the Adrians suppose. A whole new layer of life has come bubbling up and, if it's not securely on top, it's certainly fighting for the supremacy. The old ruling class England of our youth still exists, of course, but more in pockets in the country. The metropolis has certainly yielded to the invaders, and though I suppose one could still find the old nonsense talked, and the old attitudes held, in redoubts like White's or Pratt's, no one takes any notice. They aren't even worth powder and shot any more.

And I do see what Matthew is worried about. His is not a fancied dilemma, it's a real one. And it's not the least use someone like Adrian pretending it isn't there; it is. The whole tradition within which Matthew's gift operated and shone has been bundled into the background. Perhaps it's not for ever. But for the moment it

54

has been, and he is, as he says, "out". There are ways, as his advisers have found with this recital, of exploiting him and his name. But he knows very well—and he's quite right—it's not a way of using his special gift. That's the problem, and it looks pretty insoluble. Of course, it's made more acute for him that his own son should be a member of the usurping young. It brings it all home in a very sharp personal way. And this (in my view) clouds his judgement in dealing with the whole problem of Luke's "delinquency", which in any other boy of that age he would have been amused by, or anyhow, tolerant of.

But for Matthew the problem remains. If the National Theatre were a long established, and properly established, institution with a school and teaching studios of its own—as it should have—he would be one of the honorary professors, handing on his knowledge to the new generation. That wouldn't of course, be enough to satisfy him, but it would be something. He wouldn't feel, as I suspect he does now, that his talent was going wholly to waste. When I outlined this view to him he did for once listen, but pooh-poohed it, and in his Adrian voice said, "Get me teaching!" But I don't think it's

55

so silly an idea, no doubt because I've been a teacher all my life and respect it as a vocation.

But all round this problem is where the clients are such a disaster. Adrian simply refuses to see the problem as a problem. Theatrical people on Adrian's level are, of course, wildly uneducated and narrow in their interests. They don't see the problem in its general context, where it is equally hard for a writer or a painter who has fallen out of fashion, as many have in these fashion-bound days. But they can at least— given the resources—go on practising their craft. But what does an actor do without an audience? He becomes mute.

Adrian, when I made some such statement, simply denied that Matthew is "out", or anyhow not so much as he thought.

"Of course, he's not thirty-five any longer, but he's got his talent still."

But when I tried to define this: "Yes, a lovely talent but rather limited in range," he refused to look at the idea.

"Matty can do anything."

And when I demurred: "Within his rather narrow limits," there was just a wail:

"If you're not going to be more helpful than

that, you better *not* stay around." And he added," You're taking his spiel seriously."

I said: "Yes, I am. This time."

"Well, don't," he said. "Have you forgotten our Matty? Let it just flow over you!"

"Oh, I do that," I said. "But there's something in it."

"Nothing that a two years' run wouldn't cure!"

A typical Adrian view of the theatrical life. The fact, of course, is that he has no real feeling for Matty as an artist—only an admiration for him as a "success". Or am I being priggish again?

I've an idea at the back of my mind against the time, if it should come, when Matthew really faces his situation, supposing it is really as bad as I think—and perhaps he really will. A sort of Actor's Studio he might set up to keep alive his own special sort of gift and pass it on. So later, when I had the chance, I opened the subject again. He fights it, but I can see he's not entirely against it. I simply remarked apropos of his complaining about not being wanted:

"You could still teach the young a thing or two."

"Nonsense," he said, "they wouldn't listen. You don't meet the young as I do. They don't want to know."

Typical of dear Matthew to be sublimely unaware that he was talking to someone who had been a teacher and so in touch with the young for thirty-five years. I gently pointed this out and assured him from my own experience that the young are much less self-confident than they pretend to be.

"That may be true," he said, "of your science pupils and civil servants. But it's not true of the Lukes. They're as self-confident as all get-out. They know the lot. And since they're the ones the public pays to see now, they're justified by results."

I suggested that they'd soon discover how inadequate they really were and would look round for someone or somewhere to learn.

"Opera singers and ballet dancers aren't too proud to hand on all they know to the younger generation. It's one way of using one's talent," I suggested.

This did strike home for the moment. He caught alight at the idea, particularly of the ballet dancers.

"Yes, there's Sir Frederick and Sir Robert

teaching away. That's quite true. Knights both, and the Dame will join them, I suppose. Yes. There's something in that."

Then he shied away from the notion again— it is, it's quite true, unheard of in the theatrical world. But I think a seed was planted. In fact I know it was, because he made some reference to it in Adrian's presence. And Adrian, you can be sure, picked it up very smartly and asked me about it later.

"By the way, what's this idea of yours Matty mentioned?"

I said it was very vague at the moment, and probably wouldn't work anyhow.

"Then I should drop it, if I were you," he said, very tartly. "We've had quite enough of ideas that don't work, thank you."

"I WON'T take up more of your time than I have to, Sir Matthew, but I think you might be able to help us in our enquiries. About your son."

"I rather doubt it, Inspector; I and my son are not on speaking terms, and haven't been for some time."

"I'm sorry to hear that. It must be very distressing for you. The new generation are proving very difficult, aren't they?"

"They're beyond my comprehension."

"We see a good deal of it, of course. And I shouldn't be too worried. These phases pass, you know."

"Boys will be boys, I know. But I wish they'd go and be boys somewhere else."

"Somewhere else?"

"When we sowed our wild oats, we sowed them abroad—mostly—where they did less harm."

"I can imagine it's not very pleasant for you in your position to have this sort of thing all over the papers."

60

"My position? What's my position, I ask myself? 'A rogue and a vagabond' in your book, aren't I?"

"That was a long time ago, Sir Matthew."

"Pity it's not the same today, and I wouldn't have to worry."

"What I hoped you might be able to help me with is the matter of these drugs. What's his source of supply?"

"It's only hemp. It doesn't do any harm."

"No harm? I should think it does!"

"It isn't addictive."

"Not strictly, no."

"Why is it any worse than, say, alcohol then? That is addictive."

"Alcohol isn't illegal, Sir Matthew."

"Wouldn't it be wiser then not to forbid this stuff?"

"If you'd seen the sights I've seen, you wouldn't say that."

"But if it's non-addictive?"

"It is in itself, but it seems to lead on usually to other things. They start with this and, when they're immune to that, go on to the others, heroin and morphine."

"I've never tried any of them."

"I should hope not! Now, can you help me

61

at all with any suggestions about where your son might have got the stuff from? It was rather a large amount, you know. And I've reason to think it came into the country recently."

"I'm afraid not. As I've told you . . . ."

"You don't know who his new friends are?"

"Not really, no."

"I wonder if you could think a little bit, and suggest anyone; anyone at all. Anything might help."

"And have you go round and pick them up on my word?"

"Interview them, Sir Matthew, only interview them. And we wouldn't mention you, of course."

"No, I don't think I can help you, Inspector."

"You must have some idea who his friends are."

"Well . . ."

"Anything at all might help. . . . I think you must have some idea who he goes round with now. The theatre world is a small world, as I understand it, and full of gossip?"

"No, I'm afraid I can't help you."

"I think you *can*, Sir Matthew. Do you mean you won't?"

"Yes, that's just what I do mean."

"As a respectable citizen, it's your duty . . ."

"How do you know I'm respectable, Inspector?"

"Your reputation, Sir Matthew."

"That stands high, does it?"

"It could stand higher, if you'd give us the help we're entitled to."

"No, I've told you, I can't help, I'm sorry."

"Let me appeal to you in another way, as a father. . . ."

"Ah, as a father."

"Other people's sons are in equal danger of messing up their lives, unless we can put a stop to this sort of thing. As a father. . . ."

"As a father, Inspector, I'm more concerned than anything with my relations with my son. They aren't going to be improved, are they, if I'm seen to be informing on him for you?"

"In the first place there's no need for him to know."

"He's no fool, you know, Inspector."

"In the second place, isn't it only weakness to indulge him over something as serious as this?"

"I'm afraid I can't really regard it as being as serious as you do."

"I think you should."

"Naturally, it's your business to. But it's not mine. Mine, as I see it, is to try and pass the whole thing off as boyish folly and simply assume it's a phase he'll pass out of. That's how I'm treating it."

"It's my duty to tell you that your lack of co-operation is irresponsible, and it will be my duty to tell my superiors so."

"That sounds like a threat, Inspector."

"You can regard it as such if you wish to. We have been prepared to treat this case as lightly as we could on your account, Sir Matthew—to spare you embarrassment. Our representative had instructions not to press too hard. But if you're going to do nothing to help us, I don't see why we should bother to help you."

"It isn't me who's up on the charge, Inspector."

"It's you who suffer from it, I take it. Your lad doesn't seem to worry one way or the other."

"I shan't suffer much one way or the other, either. Naturally, I'm doing what I can for him."

"You may find it a good deal less easy in court, unless you're prepared to go a little of the way with us. Come, now, Sir Matthew, you must know, or have a shrewd suspicion of the crowd your son has got in with now. Even I know them."

"In that case what more do you want?"

"I may not know all of them. There may be a name or two that's escaped me."

"No, Inspector, I'm sorry. I may be old-fashioned, but I'm not prepared to help. I know nothing for certain. I should only be guessing, and I'm not prepared to throw suspicion on what may be innocent people."

"If they're innocent they have nothing to fear."

"No one is perfectly innocent. I tell you, I'm simply not playing."

"I'm very sorry to hear it."

"Still, there it is."

"Very well. But you will appreciate, won't you, that the very fact of your refusing inclines me to think that you know something that you're hiding."

"That's just typical of the law. If you're innocent you have nothing to hide, if you do hide anything you must be guilty. That's all balls, Inspector, I resent it. I hate the law."

"The law is there to protect you as much as

anyone else. Why should you be frightened of it?"

"I didn't say I was frightened of it. I said I hated it."

"I can only repeat, the innocent have nothing to fear from it."

"I can only repeat, no one is wholly innocent."

"I find your attitude very strange, Sir Matthew. Very incomprehensible."

"I can't help that, Inspector. It's your profession that makes it so, I guess. Mine gives me wider sympathies."

"Clearly we're wasting each other's time then. But it's my duty to ask you to think things over, and if you change your mind and decide to co-operate with us, you'll know where to find me. But I should do it quickly if I were you, if you don't want to find that our attitude hardens considerably."

"Thank you for your advice, Inspector. I shall bear it in mind. Let me show you out."

ACTOR'S SON ON DRUGS CHARGE

LUKE PRIOR, twenty, actor, was remanded on bail yesterday at the Bow Street Magistrate's Court on a charge of illegal possession of drugs, and of obtaining money by false pretences.

For the prosecution, Mr Ronald Atkinson said that Prior had given three "dud" cheques in the West End recently. Two were made out to well-known restaurants and were returned R.D. The third was to a jeweller for a gold cigarette case valued at £75. The defendant had then sold this case for £35, and when his cheque to the jeweller was returned R.D. the police were called in.

It was while investigating this case that Inspector Butcher interviewed Prior and had reason to believe he was under the influence of drugs. Cannabis to the value of £125 was found on him. When he was charged, Prior said: "It's quite harmless. I was taking it to a party."

For the defence, Mr Anthony Quick said that Prior admitted having the drugs on him. But he was only an intermediary: a friend had asked him to take the parcel to a party he was going to, and he had agreed to do so, not knowing what was in it.

Magistrate: Is he now saying he did not know what was in the parcel when he admitted to the police it was cannabis?

Mr Anthony Quick: He may have had a suspicion. But the parcel was wrapped. He

67

didn't think there was any offence involved in simply handing on the parcel as requested. As to the other offence, this was pure youthful carelessness. He (Anthony Quick) would call Prior's father, the well-known actor, who would tell them that he had agreed to underwrite his cheques.

Sir Matthew Prior, in the witness box, explained that there had been some misunderstanding. He was quite aware that his son was overdrawing his account, but had agreed to guarantee the overdraft. It was a secretarial error which had led to the cheques "bouncing".

When counsel for the defence opposed a remand, Inspector Butcher said that it was the drugs offence which was worrying the police. There was a lot of illegal trafficking in drugs going on in the West End and they were anxious to stamp it out. They had not concluded their investigations into this particular incident and were not satisfied that the whole truth had come out.

Bail was granted on a recognisance of £500 from Sir Matthew Prior, and Prior was remanded for a week.

DINED with Matthew. Found him in a rather more fighting mood, though still perplexed about his future. But wonderfully determined to have one. But his difficulty is real, and I wasn't much help. The fact is that after an extraordinarily lucky and extended youth, his luck has turned against him. He recognises this— that he was very lucky, and that saves him from bitterness. Of course, he doesn't naturally admit exactly how lucky he was. But he was. It wasn't merely lucky arriving at the time he did with his particular gifts, the extra stroke of luck was his beauty being so particularly photogenic so that virtually at the same time that he was making a highbrow success as a classical actor, he was also amassing a fortune from Hollywood.

He was able to play the one against the other. His classical success here gave him the right to impose the conditions he wanted on the moguls —only a limited number of films and a very stringent choice. While the financial rewards from the moguls allowed him complete freedom of choice in what he did here. He never had to compromise with mere West End successes to keep his end up. All the more surprising then that he often did.

But there is always a grave problem for the beautiful, whether men or women, as age advances. Matthew still has the features and the grace. But I think he only half realises—or is only prepared half to recognise that what has happened to him is not only the abrupt revolutionary change in the theatre. It is easier to attribute his present lack of success to that than to face that age is another cause of it. His triumphant successes were in the young parts. The adjustment to middle-aged ones hasn't by any means been either easy or very successful. Of course, he knows this in his heart of hearts. But to admit it openly would be to have to face the age problem, which is the one thing he won't face.

Or perhaps that isn't quite right. Perhaps he is slowly and painfully facing it. But he is not going to let facing it mean simply giving in to it. That's what I mean by saying he is in a fighting mood. He means to cope with it, now, perhaps for the first time. But coping with it means something different for him from passive acceptance. Where this leads him it will be interesting to watch.

There's no doubt that in the last ten years this problem has been overtaking him—catching up on him—without his perceiving it. Up till that time he was still youthful enough not to have to worry about it and, in passing, I may say that one of the things I so admired about him in his youth and up till lately was the ease and the style with which he accepted, and welcomed, success. Only a fool would think this was easy, or even usual. It is a commonplace, but none the less true for that, that success is corrupting. There are plenty of examples of that around—of people who simply couldn't and can't cope with it. They either refuse to acknowledge it—like J.O., for instance, who talks as if he was still poor when he's actually a millionaire, or R.H. who had to play the rebel all and every day—or come to that like Luke who follows in that train.

Matthew, on the other hand, always sat easily to his success and rode it both carelessly and triumphantly. He not only enjoyed it himself, thoroughly, but made sure we all enjoyed it too. He didn't have to pretend it wasn't there; he gloried in it. But what was so splendid was that he was equal to it. He could stand any amount of it without being spoiled by it. He wasn't "modest" about it, or self-depreciatory; he didn't write it off as "good luck" or a happy accident. He accepted it for what it was, not more, but certainly not less. This, in itself, is rarer than one might think, in my experience. But added to that, he made it such fun for all of us. Anyone connected with him was drawn into it and shared it with him. "Marvellous," he'd say after another success, "how the money rolls in! I shall be able to keep you all in the state to which I've accustomed you." And he did. He took the most innocent pleasure in having just what he wanted—the best of every-thing, and with such innocence that no one could find it anything but charming. And he liked nothing better, as the years went by, than showering on those who couldn't afford them the luxuries they would have liked. And some-how he managed to do it without spoiling them any more than he was spoiled himself. Well, I suppose there were a few victims, inevitably. But remarkably few.

In the early days of his first success I was the chief beneficiary. When he took a villa outside

Cannes, or a suite in one of the hotels, there was always room for me. The ticket, there and back, would always be on my breakfast plate and, once there, money would sprout in unexpected places: unexpected ways were devised to make its refusal churlish. It was part of his pleasure to see that ours was no less than his. But he had more shrewdness about money than this open-handedness suggested. In the days of comparatively low taxation, it was still possible to build up a substantial reserve, and he did. He was lucky with his investments, too—or was that part of the shrewdness?—and by the time the tax gatherers clamped down he already had a considerable fortune behind him, so that he could continue to practise the same generosity on what he made year by year without diminishing it. Some time I must try and recapture what those early days were like. It's almost impossible for anyone born into this comparatively restricted period to realise the freedom it offered when one could still go anywhere, and the pound was a really valuable commodity.

Not that, even now, it's shortage of money that restricts him, in so far as he is restricted. But that marvellous open-handedness was a condition of the complete acceptance which he

73

enjoyed. His place seemed wholly assured and unquestioned at the top of his tree, and in that world that acceptance was so peculiarly free and generous: it was his special merit that he responded to it with this equally generous attitude of his own. He was favoured of the gods and he expanded in that favour.

What exactly has caused his dethronement is an interesting and curious question. Partly, as I suggested, it is simply age. It was the young parts he was so successful in. But even more, I suppose, it's this theatrical revolution which has left him high and dry. The graces, of voice and manner, which are his special *forte*, became overnight, almost, unfashionable, and the odd thing is that the public, even his public, have gone over to the new fashion. His one attempt to join that *galère* was, not unnaturally, a stunning failure.

And the instant success which Luke had with it didn't, of course, make it any easier for him to bear. His pretence of enthusiasm never rang very true. For the moment—but I suppose only for the moment—these fashions don't last long, do they?—he's up against it. And he doesn't fool himself about it. He said last night: "Only ten years ago every up-and-coming young actor

74

could be seen and heard to be imitating me—to have taken me as their model. But now it's not me they model themselves on. That's the difference.'' He accepts it with a sort of rueful humour; but the smile is getting harder and harder to force.

JOANIE DARLING,

Have you seen me in the papers?
They've really made a spread this time. Huge
headlines. I was remanded again. I don't
mind. It keeps them on the hop. Anyhow, we
had an absurd defence. I wouldn't go, as I told
you, to their conferences to be crowed over; but
this counsel, a smoothie called Quick, caught
me before I went in and suggested I was carrying this parcel but didn't know what was in it.
I said, of course I did, and he said it was all
wrapped up, so you needn't have *known*. So that
was the line and I let them play it. It didn't
sound very convincing to me.

Actually I think the old fool of a magistrate
would have dealt with it straight away, he was
so drooling over having the great Sir Matthew
in his court, but the police insisted. They're
very hot on this drug bit. They'd had me there,
grilling me three times. Where did I get the
stuff? How much did it cost? How often had I
got it before? Did I know where I could get it

76

again? Did I realise how serious it was? Didn't I see I'd get off much more lightly if I told them? If I helped them, they'd help me. They knew I was only young and silly, just experimenting. They'ld recommend probation if I'ld just tell them . . . but if not they'ld press for the maximum. Did I know what prison was like, etc. Actually, nobody seems to get more than six months anyway. So what the hell! I'm not frightened by that. I'm not giving Jason away.

The remand suits me, anyhow. Keep things boiling, I say. Keep them on the hop about it as long as possible. It's not me they're worried about. Matthew practically admitted it in a letter he sent round by that old faggot Adrian Summers. "I don't expect you to have any feelings about me, but you might think of what it's doing to your mother." Yes, he actually had the nerve to write that! As if he cares a tuppenny fart what happens to mother. I do, as a matter of fact, so when it comes to the final showdown I'll play along with them.

Another thing Matthew said in his letter was, "Can't we get back to the relationship we used to have? Am I quite wrong in thinking that, four years ago, we were very close? I felt we were."

I dare say he did. I was a perfectly harmless

boy then, and still admired him. He could afford to flatter me by pretending to take an interest. But it's not like that now. And one can't go back.

That's what he's always trying to do, go back. Back to the time when Matthew Prior was a name to conjure with. Will he ever face the fact that it means nothing to me now? Less than nothing. Or to anyone else, except that red-faced fool of a magistrate and pink-faced Quick and other old dodderers.

The past is the past, and they live in it as if it's the present. And they won't give up. Why, for God's sake, can't he face it? He's nearly sixty and he's had it. Why can't he get out, retire, settle down in Hampshire with Mother and some dogs and give over? And write his autobiography, perhaps, quoting all those notices from the Thirties he used to bore us with?

How's everything in Nottingham? I shan't be able to get there this weekend. I suppose you can't get down, can you, for Sunday night? Do try. Why can't you cut the Monday morning rehearsal? I always did. They work you much too hard.

More love than ever,
Your own LUKE

78

"GOD almighty, they have a cheek though, don't they? Fancy seriously expecting me to go round and give Luke's pal away. . . . Not that I shall get any thanks for not doing it. In any case I rather enjoyed it, if you want to know. They're very smooth and deferential as long as they think you're one of them. But you soon see what it's like when you're on the other side. Veiled threats, false promises and moral blackmail. I even felt quite sorry for Luke yesterday in court, characteristically pert and aggressive. But you have to defend yourself somehow, don't you? . . .

"How I hated that whole episode. All that solemn paraphernalia bearing down on one poor little squit. And the smug, well-fed magistrate deferring to my title. Yes, Sir Matthew. No, Sir Matthew. I could feel Luke's contempt gimletting into my neck.

"I hate the whole thing. It's not the bad publicity that gets me, as Luke imagines. It's the whole atmosphere of a court, the police, the inexorability of it all. There's a coldness, an absence of humanity about those tiled corridors and the bleak court-room. A cruelty of exposure, relentless and implacable. It fairly puts the wind up me. I feel guilty from the moment I step into it. And the last thing I want is that anyone should ever be convicted. I'm totally on the side, in there, of the meanest sneak-thief and the nastiest of thugs. Justice is weighed against them, they haven't a chance. She has them by the scruff and she shakes them.

"The case before ours was some boys and girls arrested in the last demonstration. And you should have heard this magistrate fellow, Robertson, dressing them down as if these kids were responsible for all the evils of the moment! As if we, the middle-aged, hadn't handed them over this mess of a world to make the best of they can. If they'ld only behave themselves like sober, sensible, middle-aged magistrates, he implied, everything in the garden would be lovely! It fair turned me up. . . .

"I suppose there's no other way of doing things, but I'm sure this court business is wrong. We, the comfortably-off, middle-aged squares, put ourselves up in the form of the beak as insufferably self-righteous. What hate it must breed in the accused! Black never-ending hate, and a determination to do again whatever they did, only better next time.

"It all reminded me all too clearly of that time two young gentlemen tried to put the black on us, do you remember? Should we or shouldn't we go to the police, and how far would we be protected if we did? Luckily it never came to that. How long ago was that? Thirty-five odd years, and it seems like yesterday. We were living in that charming Swan Walk house. Wasn't that a heavenly time? Blackmail apart? And we weathered that and thought it only right that we should. How the tide was flowing with me in those carefree days! How impossible it seemed that anything could ever go wrong! And what in heaven made me decide to change my whole way of life, I simply can't imagine. It was partly your going away, I think. No, I'm not blaming you, for goodness sake. It was an irresistible opportunity you had offered. You had to take it, and anyhow it couldn't all have lasted indefinitely. It was too good to last."

"And you went and married. That I never understood."

"It was hubris on my part. I thought I could

get away with anything. The money was pouring in. Swan Walk had proved such a success. Why not a grander Swan Walk? And if so, why not a proper establishment? Why not a devoted wife, like Grace, a family, an ordered existence? No more fear of the black! And there was always dear abroad, if one wanted anything else.

"And it wasn't a failure by any manner of means, you know. The first five years were fun. Not fun like we had, it's true, pure unadulterated, irresponsible fun—or am I romanticising it? I don't think so. It was like that, wasn't it, in those early days? Everything falling into my lap, the parts, the notices, the adoration, the gallery screaming, the milling crowds outside the stage door, and the weekend parties that seemed to go on for ever. Or those dashes to Paris and holidays at Cannes? We crammed so much enjoyment into those four years that it spilled over the top and ran down the sides. Nothing could go wrong.

"What I got instead out of marriage was something else again. Respect, I suppose it was. What on earth did I want with respect, since it also meant respectability? But it *was* a compensation, sort of. No, more than that. It was acceptance in a different sphere. Our time was hectic, a kind of storm of pleasure. This was a slow steady roll carrying one securely into the future.

"I was accepted in a new way, and I liked it. And I could, I found, throw myself into the rôle of the young husband, young father, young head of a prosperous household. And I found myself being taken seriously, too seriously sometimes. That was all part of it.

"Yes, to be honest I was thoroughly flattered by this new rôle—you know how easily I'm flattered! Make no mistake, the world welcomes conformity and makes one free of its goodwill when one toes the line. And it seems worthwhile having, that goodwill, for a time anyhow. It's so much easier swimming with the current. And there's a certain self-righteousness in all of us that makes us hug that respectability and that respect. I felt very virtuous, I can tell you, for those five years. I was even ready to be snooty about those who stood outside it. I should think, looking back, that I was insufferable.

"Luke was born seven years after the marriage. He was the result of several attempts to patch up a growing split. I'm not sure Grace isn't right about that, that he's never got over it. I really think children born for that purpose are marked from the first, as if they knew already in the womb that they are only there to heal a division and that they've failed from the very start. Luke failed miserably in his initial function."

"What had gone wrong exactly?"

"I don't know. A sudden revulsion from a living lie. I was in Hollywood when I felt it, a terrible disinclination to come back, a dread of those all-too-respectable parties, a horror of domesticity, a howling need for freedom, freedom to dart away whenever the inclination took me, to do exactly what I liked exactly when I wanted to, and a reversion impossible to resist to the old temptations.

"And yet at the same time I wasn't prepared to throw it all away. The goodwill of the world that I'd so completely captured. Cowardice, I suppose. That was the time, if ever there was a time, to take the plunge back into my real world. Perhaps if any individual had come along at that time that I could take it with and for, I might have. No, I don't suppose I would. I wanted it all ways. The impossible dream. I was thirty-two, still blessedly young, but not so young as not to realise that the years for playing the juvenile rôle were closing in. The juvenile rôle not just on the stage, you understand. Off it, too. I could still manage it—just, as I discovered.

"And so the fatal compromise began. The crisis was looming in the distance. But I refused to look. Success not quite so easy to come by. Middle-age round the corner. I wasn't 'out' then. Only slipping a little. Looks going: figure thickening. But by then I had my technique perfected. I thought I could do anything and always would be able to. So I looked the other way: kept up the pretence of the respectably married man and went my own way.

"Well, there it was, and I must hand it to Grace that she stood by me over it with undiminished affection; Adrian, who's bitchy about her, says that it was just that she was bloody well not going to lose all she had got. . . . And why not? She'd a right to that feeling. But she also had thought for me. She'd save me from myself. And so through four or five years of bitterness and rows, she kept up the outward show. It took some doing. But she managed it. I did nothing to help—or very little. Just enough, I suppose, to make it possible for her.

But only just. And at the end of the time we had come—or been forced—to a sort of understanding. We kept up the front—and have kept it up ever since.

"But it just isn't possible to have it all ways, one finds. I haven't the worst of both worlds, it's true. But certainly not the best. A small piece of each, and each takes off from the other. And so it has drifted on, for how many years? Fifteen or more, and I find myself fifty-eight. And still thinking things will change. Somehow, miraculously, it will all come together without my doing anything positive about it. That's the idiotic sort of way one lives, on un-examined hope and unjustified illusions."

DEAR MATTHEW,

Luke spent a day down here and I thought you'd like to hear my impressions of him. First of all I'm *fairly* certain that he's not fallen a victim to those terrible drugs. Yet, anyhow. I think, and hope, that it's something it's thought rather *smart* to try in the circles in which he is now moving. It's a way of trying to shock us. So I'm not taking it quite so seriously as I was.

It may well be only a form of childish boasting—a form of trying to draw attention to himself (which shows, all the same, that we have both rather failed in our duty to him).

For my other impression is that he's really rather *lost*. I think he's landed himself much further *in* than he ever meant and *wants* rescuing, but, having gone in so far, can't say so.

Think of it like a child with tantrums. They, too, go much further than they mean to and then don't know how to get out of it and have to be *helped* out. I've noticed the same thing with

87

several of our difficult cases at the Youth Club.

However intelligent Luke is, he is very backward *emotionally*. And that's the very reason why I suggested that if we could make a home background for him once again—a happy home background—he would learn to grow up.

You haven't answered me about this. But I still want you to think of it very seriously. I think we should make a last effort now that we're both getting on—for *his* sake. Don't you think we've let things drift along for too many years? I warn you that I'm myself beginning to find the situation unsatisfactory.

Meanwhile I think you should really make a great effort to try and get Luke to make it up with you. He told me that you had written to him. But that isn't enough. Go and *see* him, even if it does mean pocketing your pride. I really do feel it's up to you, now, and that though he may be "difficult" on the surface, he would really welcome some advance from you.

Try! And you can't go on for ever avoiding decisions. They don't make themselves. Think over what I've said and I'm sure you'll realise it's for the best for all of us.

Affectionately,

GRACE

"COME in and sit down, Sir Matthew . . . tell me what's troubling you then."

"It's not me, Doctor, so much as my son, Luke. I don't know whether you happened to read in the papers a case he was involved in?"

"I think I did see something. Drugs, was it? Or a cheque?"

"Both."

"I see. But shouldn't he be the one who's here?"

"He should be, but he isn't, and perhaps he won't be. But I thought perhaps we could explore the ground."

"You can't persuade him to come?"

"I don't seem to be very good with him at the moment. He refuses even to see me."

"Have you any idea why?"

"Oh, I've plenty of ideas. Amateur psychology, you know. We all practise it now. You should hear my wife Grace. But I don't know that it helps much. I'm one of those improbable fathers. You must have come across them."

"No, that's a new phrase to me."

"Well, I ought never to have married, and certainly ought never to have had children."

"And you have how many?"

"Just the one. Thank goodness."

"And why do you say you ought never to have had a child."

"I don't feel responsible for him. I feel too young to be a father."

"And you're actually what, fifty?"

"Fifty-eight. So they tell me."

"Who tells you?"

"The documents, the reference books, the birth certificate. Otherwise I wouldn't believe it. You'll think that very immature, I suppose. But perhaps we actors *are* immature—and can't help being. No, I don't know about 'actors'. Why them specially? They're just like other people. There are plenty of immatures about, as you must know, Doctor. Well, I'm one of them. I'm more interested in myself than in him. It's as simple as that. But I didn't come here to talk about myself. It's Luke that's our problem."

90

"It might be more helpful if you did talk about yourself—Luke can talk about himself, if he comes."

"Oh, there's nothing wrong with me—or nothing that a thumping success wouldn't cure."

"But you're a very successful man, surely?"

"I have been. But at the moment I'm not, and we actors need success all the time. It's the only climate we flourish in. We can't be without it one day without squealing—and it isn't just neurotic, you know. Once we become uncertain of it, we become uncertain of ourselves, and that's fatal."

"And you're missing it at the moment? Or think you are?"

"I am. There's not a doubt about that."

"And you can't realise that it may be just for the moment? That it will come again?"

"I'm fifty-eight!"

"And you feel that's old?"

"Isn't it?"

"Not very, no."

"Too late to make a new start."

"But why ever should you want to make a new start? What's wrong with what you are?"

"I don't know that I do want to make a new

start. But I certainly want to be capable of it, still. Does that seem to you silly?"

"Not silly, no . . . perhaps a little unrealistic?"

"Then I'm hopelessly unrealistic. Unless I felt that possibility was boundless, that anything could be made to happen—that round the corner life was still there to start. . . . unless I felt that . . ."

"Yes, Sir Matthew?"

"I should have to admit my age."

"And would that be so awful?"

"The end, yes. The end."

"You said just now, Sir Matthew, that your son wouldn't see you. When did that start?"

"Up till sixteen or so I think he rather admired me. But we haven't communicated much for what? . . . a couple of years? Since he began growing up."

"And you can't account for that?"

"Oh yes, I can understand it perfectly. He wants to be his own success, independent of me and my name. Unfortunately he's lumbered with both."

"He could have changed the name. He's an actor, isn't he?"

"Yes, and a promising one, they tell me!"

"Haven't you seen him?"

"Oh yes, I've seen him. But I'm not a very good judge of this modern style, you know. I thought him pretty good as far as it goes."

"And did you let him see that?"

"See what, exactly?"

"That you didn't think much of his acting."

"That wasn't what I said."

"It was what you implied."

"No, no, not really. You see, I'm old-fashioned about it all. I know that. That's why I'm being left behind. This modern ill-disciplined all-over-the-place kind of thing, isn't my idea at all. But I wouldn't dream of saying so."

"I don't suppose it's difficult for him to gather it all the same?"

"Well, what do you expect me to do? Pretend I think it's all wonderful, when I don't?"

"No, the difference in how the generations regard things is always there. It's something the generations have to accept, and usually manage to, without too much friction."

"He evidently doesn't."

"Isn't it rather you who don't?"

"How do you mean?"

"Don't you refuse to accept your age and so

93

your generation, and isn't that partly what's throwing out the balance?"

"You want me simply to give up?"

"I wouldn't call accepting your age giving up."

"I would."

[*There followed then one of those long silences familiar to anyone accustomed to psychiatric sessions. But Sir Matthew was evidently not inclined to pursue the subject, and Dr Evans picked up another point.*]

"So Luke's a success?"

"Of a kind."

"A kind again you don't approve of?"

"There's this cult among the young actors of being wild, living it up, being so damned superior and intellectual and introverted that they think themselves above such elementary things as discipline. It's a cult, I know. But in my day you were sacked for it. They seem to be admired instead. Luke's in with that lot. Hence the drugs."

"How bad is that?"

94

"I haven't the faintest idea, as he won't communicate."

"Is it just marijuana or something worse?"

"Are any of them really bad, anyhow?"

"Marijuana isn't addictive; the others are."

"Cannabis was what he was accused of having."

"That's marijuana."

"It's not serious then?"

"Oh, it's serious, yes. But not disastrous."

"That's something."

"You pretend a sort of indifference to the whole question."

"Drugs have never been one of my vices. No, I'm not indifferent, really. I'm just at sea with this. It's a new world—the new generation I won't accept, I suppose you'll say. But I'm not taking a moral line about it. Who am I to do that?"

"You're his father."

"So I am!"

"And you don't think you can persuade him to come along and see me?"

"I can't persuade him to come along and see his solicitor or his barrister to talk about his defence even. He seems set on self-destruction."

"And you feel that's aimed at you?"

"Yes, really, I do. He wants to make me pay for something. The publicity doesn't hurt him. They seem to thrive on that sort of reputation. Where he's wrong is that it won't hurt me, either. I don't care if he wants to go to jug."

"It's not the best thing for your image, as they say, is it?"

"It might even make me seem less *passé*. Isn't it rather with-it to have a drug-taking son, if one can't take them oneself?"

"And you want to be thought 'with it'?"

"At my age you were going to add?"

"I didn't say it."

"You implied it! No I don't want to be with-it in that sort of way. But if I have an image which can be damaged by this, I've no business to have created it, its pure phoney."

"Why do you say that?"

"Well, isn't it? Why should I want to be thought a respectable upper-class family man? What's all that got to do with me, with the person I really am?"

"I don't know. I don't know the sort of person you really are."

"Just as well."

"Is it? Why? Why not tell me?"

*[Here there was another long
pause when the psychiatrist
thought he really might.
But no.]*

"We haven't time to go into all that now. It's Luke's problems we're supposed to be dealing with."

"Mightn't they be the same?"

"I hardly think so!"

"Well, we can't advance much further if Luke won't come to me and you won't open up with me."

"Have we advanced at all?"

"Oh, I think a little way. If Luke does come, I shall know a little about his father, anyway."

"What will you know?"

"Let me see. I shall know, shan't I, that he does feel rather guilty about the mess his son has got into, but doesn't know quite how to acknowledge that guilt. Fair?"

"Fair enough."

"Then I shall know that he does really feel that the difference in the generations is real, but won't stick by it, which is a mistake. Fair?"

"Mm."

"I shall know that there are complications in

his life which make it difficult for him to come down firmly as a father should, but which he's not ready to talk about yet. Granted?"

"Granted."

"And finally I shall know that he may be just for that very reason better able to understand Luke than Luke is prepared to realise—and that there's a real possibility of building on that."

"You always end your sessions on the hopeful note, if you can, do you, Doctor?"

"Yes, if I can, and I think I can here, don't you?"

"I'm not sure of that."

"Well, we'll see, shall we?"

DINED with Matthew again. He was in a reminiscent mood, and filled in one or two gaps about the past. He asked, did he romanticise about those early days, and I wondered. I think not. It isn't just our present age that makes them seem halcyon to look back on. They were halcyon for me anyhow. It's true I was rather a prig when I went up to Cambridge, very serious and very puritan. Somehow or other along the road I had missed out on pleasure. Being a parson's son, I suppose, with a background of good works, respectability, high thinking and plain living. I wasn't going into the Church. I was bound for teaching, but that didn't seem much different. I worked like a black my first year, and it was just as well, for when I met Matthew in my second year I had rather less time for it, though I still did pretty well.

Matthew was a revelation to me. I couldn't think why he picked on me, though I think I see now. I was a dim scholar, he was a blazing

99

social success. He was in on everything. Devastatingly handsome and with that easy manner, he charmed the birds from the trees. We met in the literary society, which he was effortlessly turning into a play-reading society, with himself, of course, taking all the leading juvenile roles. He already had his hangers-on of clients and flatterers, and it was just my refusing to join these that first attracted him, I guess.

He laid a sort of siege to me, and I, rather resenting his such easy success, to tell the truth, played hard to get. Or, it wasn't exactly playing. I really resisted. The fact was that I was terrified, terrified of enjoying myself too much. I allowed him to join me in my spartan lunches of bread and cheese and beer, knowing full well that what he usually had was pheasant and a half bottle of wine. And where all the others told him how wonderful he was, I made a lot of sharp and stringent criticisms. He munched the bread and cheese and took the criticisms seriously and came back for more. He was amused at my puritanism, and found it a sort of challenge. And having demonstrated that he could be as puritan as I was, if it suited him, braved me to prove that I could be as sybaritic as he was. Charmingly and irresistibly he introduced me to pleasure, and I soon found I had a taste for it too.

We became inseparable. In those happy days the pound stood at an absurd advantage to the French franc and one could live like a king in Paris for practically nothing. We made our first, the first of many, weekend visits there in the long vac. After our last year I had to read for a fellowship, at the British Museum, and he had been accepted as a spear carrier at the Old Vic and we set up together in a flat in Bloomsbury.

But we didn't have to do the struggling artist act. We each had an allowance from our parents —his father was a jolly stockbroker, but his mother had been on the stage, and my father was very keen on my getting a fellowship. Our joint incomes didn't amount to very much, but money went a long way in those days. We weren't flush, but we certainly had enough to enjoy ourselves, and my puritan streak was still there in the background to keep expenses down. Besides, we both were very serious indeed about our professions. I worked very hard and didn't pretend I didn't. Matthew may have given a more devil-may-care appearance. But in fact he was dead set on success and already knew, I think, that he was bound for it. It just came earlier than even he could have hoped for. He soon graduated to bit parts, and understudies thrown in. And then the lucky break came—as one felt it always would for Matthew. He was understudying Mercutio; his principal fell ill, and the second night he was on Agate happened to be in the audience.

He gave a rave notice the following Sunday. It was the lucky break-through, though success didn't come at once.

I had meanwhile failed to get my fellowship, but I got a lectureship at the LSE. Matthew handled his success with remarkable coolness. The fact being that he always had been a success, at school, at university, now here too. So it didn't throw him. He knew extraordinarily clearly even then the extent and the limit of his talent, and he designed his career to fit it exactly and bring it out to the full. Those who only saw the laughing, generous enjoyer of it all only knew a part of him. Underneath he was extremely shrewd and capable. Being accustomed to success helped him, I suppose, to be equal to this much greater success now it had come. Goodness, we enjoyed it! The move to

Swan Walk was a great success. How proud we were of that house, and how charming it was. Of course, it was all Matthew's. On my lecturer's salary I couldn't have afforded any of that. We weren't quite so equal as we had been and though he had, as I say, his marvellous gift of sharing out his triumphs and the proceeds of them in such a way that one couldn't refuse them, it wasn't *quite* the same thing for me as it had been when we were fellow students in Bloomsbury. That was *my* halcyon time.

Naturally for him it was Swan Walk, with his reputation growing, adulation on every side and the money pouring in—or so it seemed in those days. I wasn't discontented. He had taught me to enjoy, and I enjoyed, but I knew that as far as I was concerned something was over—the equality I suppose it was, and when eventually I was offered a very good post in North Africa I knew I had to accept it. It was a wrench. But a necessary one for me.

He begged me not to. Weren't we having the most wonderful time still? Wasn't life absolute heaven? How on earth could I think of breaking it up? And what was he going to do without me? It wasn't that we were still engrossed with each other. We'd got past that stage. But I was his talisman. He depended on me. But I knew he didn't. And I knew he was moving out of my world. In Bloomsbury the students I was among, and the students he was still with, mixed together on an equal footing.

But now at Swan Walk the company got grander and grander and more exclusively theatrical. My friends no longer fitted in. His took over, and the theatre became the one and only topic for gossip and discussion. Theatricals —or the theatricals of those days—hardly knew there was a world outside their narrow circle. I couldn't pretend I was so exclusively interested in who was playing what and what had happened at so-and-so's rehearsals and who was now sleeping with whom.

So I prised myself out. It was a wrench, as I say, and the more so because, as I already knew, one was really in those circles either "in" or "out". There was little chance of re-entry on odd leaves or one-night visits. And Matthew's plea that he needed me wasn't really true. He was set on his course now and nothing was going to stop him. He didn't need me any more.

I hope I don't sound bitter about it. I wasn't. Only sad. We'd had a marvellous youth—or adolescence, I should say, for we were still both of us only twenty-five. And it had come to an end—for me, anyhow. Of course I was envious that it sort of went on for him and not for me. But when I thought of the scruffy, ill-dressed, sour, resistant personality I had been when I first met him, and what pains he took to tame me, putting up with my prickles for months, I could only bless him. He had rounded out my education. But I had—and in the end we all of us only think about ourselves—learned all I could from him. It was time I got out.

[*Matthew with Stephen in his dressing room*]

"YES, I wonder about this idea of yours. An
Actor's Studio. Would it really work? Could I
really do it? Would it be any substitute for the
real thing? Or, put it this way, would it be
fun? I'm not sure it wouldn't. I'm not sure I
couldn't perhaps make something of it. It
would certainly be different. The new start?
In a sort of way, I suppose, yes. . . . But what
would they all think?

"Can I see myself at it? Yes, I think I can.
The Old Master. Don't laugh. I don't mean
anything pompous. I mean accepting my age,
accepting my distinction without fuss and without self-consciousness. Not the boring old Head-
master. Not Dr Arnold. Sort of shabby but
authoritative. Something of a Socrates figure if
you like. Accepting my age and my place: that
would be the real thing. Just what the psycho
suggested I should. Yes, I can see it vaguely.

"Of course, they'd say I was only doing it to
surround myself with handsome young men.
Not Socrates but Silenus. Well, fuck them, let

them say it. Anyhow all the best teachers have had a queer component.

"And, yes, we could make *it* different, too. The very opposite of what the term means now. We'll teach our way, our lessons, our style. Play on that, camp it up. *All forms of classical acting taught here. Artificial styles from the Greek to the Shavian particularly catered for. Rhetoric and declamation a speciality of the house. Magniloquence acquired in six weeks. Gravity guaranteed. Experts in the Heroic, the Aristocratic, the Patrician, the Courtly.* How about that? The very opposite of The Method and quite unique. Why not? What fun!

"Yet I don't know, you know. It's all very well, but would it work? Could I really carry it off? Am I really that sort of person? Or could I become it? If only I knew what sort of a person I really am! I sometimes think I'm not a person at all. Or haven't made myself one. I'm a talent. Yes, that I do know. But as a person haven't I let myself be simply created by my circumstances? Haven't I merely let myself be formed by the accidents of my life? First the young success conventionally accepting the gifts of fortune: then the English knight accepting the social conventions of the position and the title, and now drifting along on those two pasts and avoiding being a person at all. I don't choose a path. I accept the one that's there. I never have to make a decision over anything that matters. I don't live. I exist. And isn't it too late now to make the effort?"

*PART
TWO*

PART
TWO

[Matthew and Adrian in the Albany flat]

"THANK God you've come. I've got myself into a hell of a mess. And I don't quite see how I can get out of it. Christ, what have I done?"

"Take a drink duckie, and take it slowly and tell me just what's happened."

"I got rather high tonight. Well, more than high. And it wasn't only drink.

"Those reefers you got for me. I tried one. It was a very odd sensation—a don't-care-a-damn-for-anyone feeling, a detachment from reality, a sort of floating, and a certain sexual excitement. You can guess what I did next?

"Well, I did. I got myself up in all my gear and went out—in the car—and had an accident.

"It wasn't bad. I hit an island, broke the glass and the light, and as ill-luck would have it there was a copper down the road. You can imagine my predicament. There I was in full drag. I didn't know what to do."

"What did you do?"

"What I was told. 'I must ask you to

III

accompany me to the police station.' I wasn't very steady on my feet.

"And then I behaved like a fool. I suppose it was that stuff, and the copper, very polite, calling me 'Madam'.

"Well, what was I to do? Say I'm really Sir Matthew Prior? They treated me as a woman, for God's sake. They all thought I was one. So I called myself Mrs and no one thought different. You see how awkward it was, don't you? Once I'd started I just had to go on with it. Then I was charged with driving under the influence. I hadn't got my licence or insurance so there was nothing to show. I've got to surrender to my bail in the morning. What do I do then, for God's sake?

"And what was I to say when the sergeant asks, 'Will you submit to the usual tests, Madam?' I was so far in by then there was no going back. I said, 'Don't bother, I admit it. I've had too much to drink and I oughtn't to have been driving.' I couldn't have a police-woman watching me pee, could I? I refused to take the tests—but I signed a statement. But, of course, it was in this false name and address. I can't get away with it, they've got the number of the car. They'll be round in no time. And then, you see, they examined my bag, and I'd popped the two spare reefers in, and they got on to those at once."

"I must say, ducks, this time you have over-done it."

"What the hell am I to do?"

"Get hold of Cruddle, now."

"I've done that. He's on his way up from Wimbledon or wherever it is he lives. . . . But I don't look forward to that!"

"How do you mean?"

"Giving myself away to him."

"There's no need to. We can think of some-thing. . . . I was giving a party. You were coming round to give one of your female impersonations. How about that?"

"Pretty thin."

"We can work it up. You're famous for your female impersonations. We can all swear to that."

"Why didn't I say that at the time?"

"That was the demon drink."

"I suppose we can try it. I carried the joke too far? What with the drink and the hemp? I suppose they may believe it. . . .

"We can try it. Try it on Cruddle. See how he reacts. God, the follies one commits, and just at this time. . . .

"With Luke in the shit, and me supposed to be helping him out of it. I knew something like this would happen. Directly I got involved with solicitors and police and all. It was bound to. I could feel it in the background all the time. Not Luke, but me. There in the·dock. And there I bloody am. This will really be the end of me."

"Now, now, it's not too bad."

"'Famous Actor on Vice Charge.' How much worse can you get?"

"I'm sure we can square that part."

"Inspector Butcher's no fool, you know."

"It may not be him."

"Fate saw to that. It was Bow Street, of course, and Inspector Butcher's already taken an ugly against me. No, he'll want his pound of flesh. Make no mistake about that."

"I'm sure we can work all that, if we all rally round."

"And just suppose we do. Let's suppose Inspector Beastly really has a heart of gold—as if that's likely—and says, oh, yes, of course, you were going to a party to give female impersonations. What could be more natural! Let's make that highly unlikely supposition. I'm still left with the drugs, and with Luke already up on a charge. It's not going to look very pretty is, it? I'll have to warn Grace, shan't I?"

"She'll stand by you."

"Oh, of course, doing the noble, piling guilt on guilt. And if it comes out—the worst, I mean, how they'll gloat. They know already, I suppose. It's common gossip, I expect.

"Well, it was bound to happen one day, wasn't it? I must count myself lucky to have steered clear so long. But oh, the folly of it, the folly of it. . . . I don't think I can face it. I really don't. Isn't it better to get out, disappear? That's where Oscar was such a damned fool. He had the chance and didn't take it. What happens if one skips? I must ask Cruddle. They wouldn't pursue me, would they? It's not serious enough for that. I wasn't doing any harm—to anyone else. Christ, what madness! What possessed me? And if one goes, what happens to one then? How does one live? What sort of life would it be? Drink and the queer bars. Horror, sheer horror! No, that's no good. But what do I do? Just what the fucking hell do I do now?

"I'll have to disappear. Of course I shall. Let's face the facts. It's the complete end for me. Is even Darby and Joan possible now? In respectable Hampshire? Certainly not. No, it's round the world with Grace under a false name in a cruise liner; and not even the Captain's table ... where's that blasted Cruddle? Why doesn't he come? ... No it's not that either. I'm not going to spend the rest of my life being forgiven by Grace. Stuff that for a lark. It's Tangier, I suppose, and expatriate drunks and ageing cast-offs. Myself not least. I'll get Stephen to come with me, all expenses paid like the old days. Only not like the old days because we're fifty-eight, washed up and in disgrace. God fuck everything to hell. Where's that blasted Cruddle?"

[*Sir Matthew and Cruddle in Albany*]

"THIS must be pretty serious, getting me up at this time of night. What's your juvenile delinquent been up to now?"

"It's not Luke this time, Cruddle. It's me. I'm in a jam."

"What have you been doing?"

"Drunk while driving."

"Oh Lord. Have you admitted it?"

"Yes. . . . I had a little accident."

"How bad?"

"Not too bad. No one hurt—an island damaged."

"No, that's not too bad then. You'll get off with a fine and a suspension, I expect."

"But that wasn't all. At the station they found some hemp on me."

"What on earth were you doing with that?"

"What does one do with it? Smoking it, of course."

"Well, well, well. . . ."

"Shocked?"

"It's no use my being shocked. The question is how we defend it."

"We condemn the boy for doing it, and we don't even know what it's like. What *is* the attraction? I wanted to find out."

"That was very foolish of you, if I may say so, very. Still, it does give us a line . . . we'll need Quick, of course. He'll be able to make something of that, I dare say. But it'll only be mitigation, you understand?"

"What are the penalties?"

"It could be prison. That's a possibility you must face. But in the circumstances, with Quick on form . . . a thumping fine, I imagine."

"That isn't quite all."

"Not something worse?"

"Possibly. You see I was going to this party where I was going to do one of my turns. You haven't seen me do one of my turns, have you?"

"No."

"You'ld enjoy it. They're said to be quite funny."

"And so?"

"Well, I was all dressed up for it, you see . . . in the car . . . to save time . . . when I was arrested . . . I was in this disguise."

"And you explained?"

"No, well, I didn't, you see. I wanted to see if I could carry it off. Half that, half panic, I suppose. With the hemp, you see . . ."

"You didn't tell them who you were?"

"No, I gave a false name."

"What?"

"Mrs Francis."

"*Mrs* Francis?"

"My turn is a female impersonation, you see. Rather convincing it is."

"You were dressed up as a female and you didn't tell them? You kept it up and they believed you?"

"Rather a triumph, wasn't it?"

"It may be a very costly one."

"I've got to surrender to my bail in the morning and take my driving licence and my insurance round within five days. What shall I do? Dress up again?"

"You'll never get away with it."

"You haven't seen me in my drag."

"For God's sake, Prior, you're in enough trouble. Don't mess about with this."

"I was only joking."

"This is no time for jokes."

"Presumably you can take it up with them and explain?"

"Hm. I think it would be better if you did. They aren't going to like being made fools of. Which station?"

"Bow Street."

"That's our friend Inspector Butcher then. He's a very reasonable fellow, very decent sort of man. I'll make an appointment for you and you go round and make a clean breast of it."

"Unfortunately, Butcher came to see me about Luke. We didn't get on very well. In fact we loathed each other."

"That's a pity. But I don't see any alternative."

"*You* couldn't do it?"

"I could. But it wouldn't be the same thing. No, I think you must go yourself. It's your best chance."

"But there's nothing . . . criminal about this, is there?"

"Impersonating a female in public? There might be. In any case, it's not going to look very healthy for you, is it . . . if they pressed it. And there's giving a false name."

"Is that an offence?"

"No, but it makes it worse."

"You are gloomy."

"It's a gloomy situation, Prior, I don't mind

telling you. It's all going to look bad, very bad. And I must say I think you've behaved with unparalleled stupidity."

"Don't you start lecturing me. Leave that to the beak."

"The only thing we can do is to take things one at a time. The drink and the . . . er . . . hemp, we can't wriggle out of, if you've admitted it. We'll have to face them when the time comes. But first let's try and get this other matter out of the way. Will you see Butcher? I'm sure that would be best."

"I suppose I shall have to."

"I'll fix it up then, and let you know; you'll be hearing from me in the course of the morning. I don't think there's anything else we can do."

"What's the penalty for masquerading as a female?"

"That would only be a fine. And of course if the magistrate believed your story of a party and female impersonations and all that . . ."

"Why shouldn't he?"

"I think he would, I think he would. But the point is this: the police aren't going to like having been made fools of. If they turned nasty they might try and put a sinister interpretation on it. There are people, you know, who can't resist this sort of thing."

"Are there?"

"Indeed there are. And then it might be a question of importuning—and all sorts of unpleasant suggestions could be made. I don't say there will be, and I don't say they'll be believed. If it's Robertson on the bench again, he's a sound man and would no doubt believe you. In your position and all, and being an actor. But the suggestions would have been made, the smear would be there. Mud would be flung and . . ."

"Mud sticks."

"Exactly. I don't like it. I don't like it at all. The publicity might be very damaging. As it is, it's bad enough. Drugs and drink and driving. And then there's illegal possession, isn't there? You say they found some on you?"

"Yes, in my handbag. . . ."

"Handbag, Prior? Really!"

"Well, there it was, there was no denying it. I finally signed a statement."

"I'm not sure that was very wise."

"Well it was either that or taking a test, and I couldn't do that, could I, with a wpc watching?"

"You refused to take the tests?"

"I had to."

"Then that's another offence. Do you realise that?"

"Not the most serious in the circumstances, is it? I signed a statement."

"You admitted everything?"

"Not everything, did I? Only the drink and the drugs."

"That's bad enough in all conscience. As to the other, it just depends how Inspector Butcher feels about it."

"He can see a joke surely?"

"We can all see jokes when they're practised on other people. It's another matter when we're the victims. We'll just have to do the best we can. But let me beseech you, Prior, to go round to Butcher with your tail between your legs."

"That's just where it is at the moment. Don't worry."

"Don't try and be funny with him, I tell you, they're not going to like it. But he's a sensible chap."

"That's not quite what I found last time. I thought him a bit of a bully."

"All I can say is, don't give him the chance

to bully you again. Do whatever he asks . . . otherwise . . ."

"You'll make an appointment for me?"

"First thing in the morning. I'll be in touch. And I'll contact Quick. We'll need him."

"Thank you for coming. I was rather panicky."

"You might well have been. And you did right to send for me straight away. Goodbye for the moment."

WOKEN up last last night by the telephone.
Adrian. Could I come at once! Matthew in
deep trouble. So, of course, up I got and
dressed and went round.

And it does look very nasty, I must say. I had
rather thought that this aberration of Matthew's
belonged to his youth and had been given up.
Apparently, not entirely. But it was, it seems,
confined to the privacy of his own home and
only a very few very select friends ever saw it in
operation. I rather blame myself for never
having taken it very seriously. When we were
young, it just seemed an amusing camp
addition which he indulged for the pure joke
of it, since he made a rather fetching girl. I
hadn't really imagined it to be an obsession,
which it evidently is, since all these years he has
collected more and more gear.

But then as he talked about it, it became
clear that neither had he. He had really supposed that with his marriage he was going to
change. "I thought", he said "that I could, so

to speak, just 'put away childish things' and grow up by an act of will. As if the boys and the parties and the dressing up were only youthful fun and games that one could put behind one. I was very naïve, I suppose. But it seemed to work, for a time, you know, and there were all the compensations of respectability, which aren't to be despised. But it just didn't work for very long. But even then I did have the wits to be sensible. This is literally the first time I've gone out in public like that since our early days in Paris. The very first time, and this would happen!"

How serious it is, or will be, it's hard to say at this point. In the early hours it seemed pretty grim. We did discuss one other possibility—that he should use that old parking offence device and report his car as stolen and simply never turn up at Bow Street. But in the end—I think wisely—Matthew turned it down. "To start with it's the oldest trick in the business and they must know it as well as we do. And then if they got on to it—and I bet they would—I really would be deep in the soup. At least if I try and face it out with Butcher, it'll look as if I've nothing to hide. Whereas if we tried to work this and it failed, I should pronounce myself guilty at once."

Anyhow, there we were talking round and round it till at last, at four in the morning, Matthew was persuaded to take a sleeping pill, and I went off and did the same. Not that it did much good—or his for him, I suspect. The horror went round and round in one's head as it does on these occasions. All we can do is to trust to Matthew's luck, and he is, as some are and some aren't, a naturally lucky person.

I can't believe that his whole career is going to be brought to a squalid close in this sort of way. Were we perhaps in the night exaggerating the effect it might have? How seriously would people take something like this? Might they not, nowadays, just laugh and forget it? Given a year or so anyhow?

But that's to forget the kind of crisis in which Matthew feels himself anyhow. Even if the world was merely amused, he wouldn't be. For him it will be only a violent intensification of the mess he feels he's in. Is my suggested solution impracticable now, if a public scandal ensues? It certainly won't make it easier.

"MR CRUDDLE tells me that you have something you want to straighten out with us."

"Yes I have."

"I hope I can guess what it is."

"I don't suppose you can. You've got a rather odd case on your hands. Driving under the influence—a Mrs Francis."

"Ah, yes, rather puzzling. You know her, I suppose. She was driving your car, I believe."

"You see, I'm the Mrs Francis in question."

"Perhaps you'd better explain a little further."

"It's perfectly simple. I was going to a party to do my party turn—a female impersonation. I'm rather well known for it. And I bumped into this island thing. One of your fellows picked me up, and I couldn't resist—I know it was foolish—carrying the impersonation through. He took me for a real woman—so did your desk sergeant. So I didn't disabuse them. I gave the first name that came into my head. . . . It was silly, wasn't it? It seemed funny at the time.

128

Do you understand? But I see it wasn't as funny as I thought. And I've come to make a clean breast of it."

"Did it seem funny at the time, Sir Matthew, because you were under the influence? Is that what made it seem funny?"

"I wasn't drunk, but I had had a drink or two."

"If I remember rightly, in the case of Mrs Francis there was both drink and drugs, wasn't there? Weren't some reefers found in her handbag?"

"Yes, I'm afraid some were."

"And she refused point blank to take tests, as I recall?"

"But you see why that was. She wasn't in a position to, not being a real 'her'. She signed a statement."

"Under a false name with a false address. So at best that's not worth much."

"But you understand about it now?"

"Oh, I think I understand about it, yes."

"So where do we go from here?"

"What do you propose, Sir Matthew?"

"Well, I rather hoped we might forget about the false name and all that, and start from there."

"Yes, we could do that. We could do that . . . on certain conditions, of course."

"What would they be?"

"Of course, I should have to have a full statement now, admitting the offences, the drink that is and the drugs, under your own name."

"I can hardly refuse that in the circumstances, can I? Of course, I'll sign anything."

"Good, that takes care of that then."

"I take it, by the way, that this conversation is off the record?"

"If it weren't there'd be a shorthand typist taking down all you say. That only comes after you're charged."

"And I shall be charged, of course?"

"At the moment Mrs Francis has been charged. Whether you come forward to answer that charge is up to you."

"But I thought we'd disposed of that problem now."

"Not entirely, Sir Matthew, not entirely."

"I don't get it, Inspector."

"Don't you, Sir Matthew?"

"I'm quite ready to sign a confession, a statement, whatever you call it. It's not much good not, is it?"

"As the marijuana was found in Mrs Francis's bag and you admit to being Mrs Francis, I should say not. So that's the first thing. But it's not quite all."

"I've brought along my driving licence and insurance if that's what you want?"

"Yes, we have to have those. . . . Thank you. . . . But not, I see, in the name of Mrs Francis. . . ."

"You're beginning to worry me, Inspector."

"I don't think you've any need to worry, Sir Matthew. I'm a reasonable man if I'm treated reasonably."

"I get a faint whiff of blackmail, Inspector."

"You won't do yourself any good by making accusations, Sir Matthew. If you don't intend to co-operate, I don't quite see what you've come for."

"I came to make a clean breast of a silly joke I played on your men. Can't we get that over with?"

"I don't know that it's all quite as simple as that. Impersonating a female in public and giving a false name."

"My information is that no offence has been committed by giving a false name."

"I didn't say that any offence had been

committed by the act of giving a false name—even false as to its sex. I just said that it wasn't quite as simple as all that."

"Don't you accept my explanation?"

"It's not a bad explanation, I'll admit. Whether I accept it or not is another matter . . . Strictly, it's anyhow irrelevant what I accept or don't accept. Will the magistrate accept it?"

"I think so, yes."

"So do I. It's only a pity it has to go as far as that, isn't it? You know what the newspapers will make of it?"

"I should have thought a man of your experience could see that it's obviously the truth."

"A man of my experience comes across some very odd bits of behaviour, Sir Matthew. Nothing surprises me. And in my experience the combination of drink *and* drugs has a curious effect. It often brings out these bits of odd behaviour which respectable men like to keep hidden—if they can. That's what my experience tells me."

"What do you propose to do then?"

"You accuse me of blackmail—a very ugly word, when all I was suggesting was a bargain. I'm prepared to believe—or rather shall I say

132

accept—your story about the impersonation. But what *quid* do I get for my *quo*?"

"That marijuana in my bag, I could tell you where I got it."

"I see. But you must understand that the information would only be interesting to me if the stuff came from an unusual source. If all you're going to tell me, for instance, is that you bought it off a stranger in a pub in the Tottenham Court Road—well I know that source of supply without your telling me."

"That's exactly where I did get it."

"So I suspected—from the fact that it was done up in reefers. But now the stuff your son Luke was found with was a sizeable block. That came from somewhere else, somewhere abroad, I suspect."

"I see. So we're back where we started the other day?"

"Not quite, Sir Matthew, not quite. There's a new factor in the equation now, isn't there?"

"Is there?"

"Surely? Mrs Francis, eh?"

"My God, yours is a dirty job, Inspector."

"You respectable people are all alike. You want crime cleared up, but you don't want to know how it's done. When you're dealing with criminals and shall I say . . . perverts, you can't afford to be Simon pure."

"I've told you already I'm not acting as a police informer over my son."

"That's what you told me the other day. But the circumstances now are rather different. Don't you think you would be wise to reconsider?"

"What would your superiors say if I told them of this conversation?"

"As I remarked before, this is entirely off the record. I could simply deny it. But if you ask me, my superiors might take the line that I was being too generous. They might, for instance, ask why I didn't press the Mrs Francis business a little harder. They might ask why, if you had this perfectly acceptable explanation of your attire, you didn't offer it at the police station. I think they might regard that as a rather suspicious circumstance. But I'm not pressing it—at the moment."

"Not if I come clean?"

"Let me spell it out. I'm quite prepared to accept your explanation of the Mrs Francis episode to the extent of pretending it never happened. I'm prepared to accept a signed statement from you in your own name, and I won't have the question of any female impersonation brought up if you in return will give me the information about where your son was getting his supply of drugs from."

"I've told you, I'm not even certain."

"I suggest you could find out, if you wanted to. Think it over. There's no hurry. The wheels of the law grind slowly, though, need I remind you, they grind exceeding small, if they have to. Go away and consult your Mr Cruddle. He's a very sound man. And let me know what you decide. Don't leave it too long, of course. What shall we say, a couple of days? And believe you me, you'll be doing your duty as a citizen *and* a father, if you help us."

"I can tell you now, Inspector. I simply couldn't do it. How could I?"

"Don't tell me anything now, Sir Matthew. I don't want to rush you. Take my advice, go away and think it over. Face your position. It's not very healthy. You were out in public dressed as a female under the influence of drink and drugs. You say you were going to this party to give female impersonations, but you might find yourself pressed in court to explain why you didn't give that perfectly acceptable explanation at the police station. In cross-

examination it might be made to sound rather
. . . what shall I say? . . . ugly. Now all I want
is some information which I rather think you
can give me. But which no one—and I repeat
no one—need know came from you. Think it
over, will you? And don't say anything now.
Let me know what you decide in a day or two."

[*Matthew and Stephen in the Albany flat*]

"WHY is it I always seem to be in some dilemma? Can you answer that? Why can't life be as straightforward for me as it is for everybody else? What have I done to deserve it? Perhaps to other people it would all seem simple enough. A simple choice of my future or somebody else's. It isn't even as if it's Luke's actually, though we don't know how much of the original responsibility was his, if it came to close enquiries. They tell me you can pay for this stuff in London and get it smuggled in. This Jason Squire fellow brought it in, but did Luke order it? Once they start enquiring, where will it end? But at the moment it's me or Jason Squire and who is Jason Squire?

"As far as I know, just a photograph in the papers, a pin-up boy. 'What's Jason Squire to me or me to Jason Squire, that I should weep for him?' Why, then, do I find this deep reluctance in myself to give his name away? Is it just obstinacy, just that hatred of the law that we who've been on the wrong side of it all these years inevitably feel? It's not loyalty, certainly. I owe him no loyalty. I owe him nothing. He seems the sort of young man who can look after himself. I just say those two words, Jason Squire, and I'm off the hook. Why then do they stick in my gullet? I want to be off the hook, don't I? And I'm off it, for two words. Two words I can't say. But should I make myself? That's the question. And I'm damned if I can find the answer. To ask the hard question is simple, Auden says somewhere. Profoundly true. It's all questions without answers, all along.

"Why should I be in this predicament anyhow? Is it my fault? Fundamentally? Wasn't I born with this kink? I certainly never wanted it. Some are born with crooked noses, humped backs, protuberant eyes. My nose is straight, my back upright, my eyes one of my features. But I dress up. Don't ask me why. The hard question simply asked. There it is.

"What would the psycho have said if I'd asked him? Something like this: My father was a repressed womaniser with a frigid wife. He wanted a daughter desperately. I wanted his regard desperately. So I must play the girl to get it. All right. Suppose that's the answer, slick though it seems to me. Knowing the cause does nothing to eradicate the disease. I tried anyhow, didn't I? God knows I tried. If an act of will could change one's direction, my marriage would have changed it. But in these things the will is unimportant. I might as well have been born with it for all I can do to help it. Control it then. Easier said than done.

"Besides, it made me an actor, I suppose, dressing up, in the first place. It's got me where I rather miserably am. Where I am in life, where I am today. With the two liberating words, Jason Squire, stuck in my gullet.

"Hell and damnation, what shall I do? Tell me, someone. How wretchedly impoverished we are without a bloody God to turn to. Alone, on a cooling planet, with only ourselves to help ourselves. I used to believe all that humanist guff about the grandeur of man facing his own destiny. It isn't true. We need Belief. All of us, desperately. The lack of it is driving us from dust to ashes. But there it is: we can't have it for the asking. They've walked out on us, the gods, and they won't come back, not in our era.

"So who can tell me what to do? Only my weak and foolish self. And what do my weakness and my folly say? For some unaccountable reason, it seems to say: 'You can't do it. *That*, you can't do.' Why, tell me why?"

"I can't tell you why. I don't understand it."

"Don't you? Do you really not? To me it seems as plain as plain. That I can't do. If I'm wrong, tell me."

"You risk your whole future, your whole career."

"What future? What career? Can you answer *that*? If I thought I had a future, if I thought my career mattered any more, it might be different. But I'm not sure it would be even then. But having neither, neither future nor career, how can I justify putting someone else in the shit just to save my ageing hide? That's what it boils down to. Me or him. It's as simple as that. But how simple is that? It isn't simple to me. As I say, I don't know. I haven't often bothered about other people. I don't seem to have had to. And it's not him I'm really bothering about even now, do you understand that? It's me again. What sort of person am I? What can I and what can't I do? And I'm damned if I know the answer."

MATTHEW still hovering between decisions. But looking more and more like coming down on the side of letting the worst happen if it has to. Grace got nowhere with him and retired to Hampshire in a huff.

Today he meets the lawyers—or Quick, rather, who is going to have a last bash at convincing him. He's a highly intelligent man, much more sophisticated, of course, than old Cruddle. I happened to be at Matthew's yesterday when Cruddle brought Quick round for a preliminary talk. Matthew was late, as usual, and I was amused to hear them discussing the case off the record so to speak. Quick asked Cruddle what he thought of Matthew's story of the impersonation. And Cruddle, who is really rather sweet but an intellectual buffer, said with absolute sincerity and loyalty that of course he accepted it. Quick gave him an amused smile and said it didn't ring very true to him. Cruddle seemed genuinely surprised. It was obviously the first time he had thought of questioning it.

"If you or I were going to a party dressed up to give female impersonations and this happened, what would be the first thing we'ld do. Tell them who we were and promptly, eh?"

Cruddle looked very perplexed at this: "He says that was the drink and the hemp."

"Seems more like guilt to me," Quick said cheerfully.

This time Cruddle was shocked. He couldn't believe something like that of Sir Matthew Prior. "He seems such a nice chap."

"Even 'the nicest chaps' have their quirks," Quick said blithely.

"Yes, but this . . . !" Cruddle protested.

"It's surprising how common it actually is," said Quick; and when Cruddle protested that this was an exaggeration he proceeded to treat us to an animated disquisition on the subject, bringing in pantomime, folk lore, dirty stories, of which he told several, and finally Shakespeare. "Some pretty larks they got up to, there. And what about your children? Weren't they continually swapping sex rôles when they were young? I know mine were."

142

Cruddle, of course, wouldn't have noticed it even if his had.

"And when all's said and done," Quick concluded, "I don't know why we make such a fuss about it. It's innocent enough in itself."

But when they went on to discuss whether or not on this occasion a fuss would be made, Cruddle thought it would. Butcher was a tough man when crossed, he said, and Quick said that in that case Matthew must bow to the inevitable and tell him what he wanted to know, and was, at that time, fairly sure that he would. What else could he do? But now they're not so sure and Quick is having another go tomorrow.

*[Quick and Sir Matthew in Quick's chambers in
Gray's Inn]*

"Aн, Sir Matthew, there you are, come along
in. Cruddle and I have been going over this
affair and we think we've come up with a fairly
sound solution. It won't be half as bad as you
think, if you'll just take our advice."

"I hope it's better advice than the Inspector's,
that's all I can say."

"Cruddle says he's pretty straight. He'll play
straight with you if you play straight with
him."

"Well, I don't think I will."

"I really can't believe that. It's a most
reasonable arrangement, you know."

"It's nothing less than blackmail. They're all
the same, these policemen, judges and magistrates. They aren't interested in the truth."

"Not in that sense, no."

"Well, I'm not interested in their bargains
and evasions and arrangements. I've got more
important things to worry about."

"Such as?"

"Such as—I've not made much of a success of my rôle as a father. I don't suppose I ever shall either. I'm an improbable father, Quick, most improbable. All the same, there are limits. What they're asking me to do is deliberately inform on my son. I don't see how I can do it. He's not done anything very much, anyhow. Good God, what's a puff or two of marijuana in the world we live in?"

"That's all very splendid, Sir Matthew. Very splendid indeed. But you are evading the real problem. The problem is very precise, and it is entirely technical. As parents, husbands, citizens, we may have all sorts of points of view which might or might not be different from your own. But I'm here as a lawyer. We're faced with a technical legal problem and I have produced a technical legal solution. The question is a quite simple one: are you prepared to put aside for a moment your sentimental, or shall we say moral, view of your situation and address yourself to the legal aspect?"

"They're all mixed up. You can't separate them."

"You mean *you* can't. I can. That's my job and I've prepared your case, when you're ready to listen to it."

"Carry on then."

"You, at the height of your career, are in some real danger of bringing it to a rather sensational stop. If the prosecution choose to make a lot of innuendos about female impersonation combined—combined, as I say, with the taking of drugs, they will be able to get you at the very best such adverse publicity as to endanger your career. We may, or may not, be able to mitigate the actual charges, but we can't prevent the more scurrilous newspapers making hay with your reputation. By the time they've finished with you, it'll be perhaps a good many years before you appear in public again. Do you think that's a fair statement of your position at the moment?"

"I suppose it may well be, but on the other hand . . ."

"Wait a minute. Grant me I'm not exaggerating, and let's see where we go from there. Let's suppose, just suppose, that somehow or other we can get them to drop the female impersonation part of the story which you must see is very damaging to the whole notion of you as a respectable family man. . . ."

"Which I'm not. . . ."

"Which as far as the magistrate and the jury

146

—if it comes to a jury—are concerned, you *are*. To them you are a highly respected member of a profession which is now perfectly respectable. You are a father, and an injured father—for your son has got himself into trouble for, among other things, trafficking in drugs. Now how does this injured father behave? Does he fly into a passion and threaten to cut off his son and never see him again? Does he play the heavy father? Not a bit. The very opposite. He wants to help, he wants to understand. He desperately wants his relationship with his son to be a better one, a more helpful one. He wants to show that son that he is not the old-fashioned heavy father. He wants to demonstrate it. To prove it. He is not going to be accused by that boy of being a square who refuses his sympathy and his understanding. So what does he do? He deliberately, and knowing what he is doing, sacrifices himself for that son. He makes himself the subject of an experiment, a guinea-pig. Although he has, only naturally, never taken any drugs himself—in fact he detests the idea of drugs—he tries for himself the experience of smoking marijuana in order to understand what the attraction is. Then, with that experience behind him, he will be in a far better position—

so he argues—to remonstrate with the boy. He may have been right in his reasoning, he may have been wrong. But what is certain is that he did this for the best of motives.

"Well, we know what happened next. The drug was more potent than he bargained for. It diminishes, he discovered, the sense of responsibility to an extent he hadn't anticipated. And under its influence he drove his car and collided with an island. Fortunately there was little damage done. And he has certainly learnt his lesson. He admits freely to the charge of driving while under the influence and of illegally possessing the drug. But he asks you to take into account the reason why he originally experimented with it. He now sees that this was probably a mistaken attitude. He certainly has learned of the dangers of this terrible habit and is in a position to do his utmost to discourage anyone from experimenting with it in the future. But he was only acting for the best as he then saw it, and I hope you will think this mitigates the offence which he freely admits. . . . How does that strike you?"

"It's simply not the truth!"

"You won't face facts, Sir Matthew. We are not dealing with the truth *sub specie aeternitatis*, we're dealing with legality, and a technical legal problem. It's your decision; I can't do more than put the position to you as I see it and take your instructions. But if I'm to conduct that defence properly you'll have to bow to the inevitable and tell Butcher what he wants to know. We've really got to get this wretched female impersonation business out of the way. That's the first thing."

"I tell you I haven't made up my mind about that yet, but as for that defence of yours, I don't want any part of it. Don't think I don't admire your skill. I think it's most ingenious and would probably work."

"Then why not take advantage of it?"

"Look, for God's sake, you know perfectly well, and Butcher knows perfectly well, if you don't, what I was dressing up for that night. And I'm asked to turn informer if I want that charge dropped. And when that shabby bargain has been transacted, you want me to sit there in public while you present me—and I allow myself to be presented—as a model father grieving over his lost son and sacrificing himself to help him. When you know and I know that I don't give a fuck about the poor little brute one way or the other, and don't think he's done anything wrong, anyhow. I'm simply not going on record as a respectable bourgeois horrified by the drug menace and ready to persecute every young man who tries a puff. I'm not like that. I think they're being idiotic over this whole thing. And I simply won't ally myself with them over it."

"Don't you think you'ld be wise to think it over? Sleep on it, eh?"

"I don't need to think this over, anyhow. I see what you call the technical problem and I see that as far as you're concerned it doesn't matter a damn whether it's true or not. You do this one technically brilliant job and then turn on to the next. But I—I have to live with what you've done for the next however many years. I have to live with turning informer and then using Luke's case to slither out of my own. It stinks; and this last I know I won't do."

"In that case what are your instructions for me?"

"We'll play along with the party and my female impersonations. I'd better stick to that lie now I've started it. Make the most you can of that."

"As I told Cruddle, the magistrate may well accept it. It sounds plausible except for one thing. Why didn't you give that explanation at the police station?"

"I know, I know. You must do the best you can with it."

"And the marijuana?"

"Plead whatever mitigation you can think up, if there is any. But don't try and shelter me behind Luke."

"It's not much to go into court with. But if that's what you want. . . ."

"That's what I want."

"And we'll pray for you when the cross-examination starts."

[*From Stephen Luther's diary*]

MANY comings and goings, to-ings and fro-ings,
arguments and counter-arguments about what
poor Matthew should do now. It's really rather
an appalling decision for him and I'm blessed
if I know just how I should act in his circumstances. Adrian is quite sure: "If it's him or me,
I should choose me." But, of course, it is not as
simple as that in any case. Once Matthew gave
the name away, investigations would start, and
one doesn't know how far they would go or
what they would reveal.

But I don't think this point weighs with
Matthew very strongly. I think he probably
doesn't know just what is weighing with him
exactly. But I believe myself that there's some
very strong undercurrent working below the
surface, made up partly of guilt, I suppose, but
partly of—mostly of, perhaps—a determination
to change his life. This crisis has brought to a
head all the discontent that was suppurating
under the skin. He has been facing more
squarely the years of evasion and liking them

less and less. A further evasion now would kind of epitomise his whole policy of evasion, and that's what he means by saying he's reached his sticking-point.

It isn't so much a moral stand he's taking *vis-à-vis* the outside world. It's rather a moral stand against his own inner weakness, his long compromise with his life.

Because I see this, or think I do, I'm accused, of course, of aiding and abetting him, of positively encouraging him. "I don't trust you, ducky," was how Adrian expressed it. We were talking over the possibility—which I suppose is really there—that one of us who knew the person involved should go round to Butcher and tell him who it was. Adrian wouldn't, of course, have the moral guts to do it. "It would be as much as my life was worth," he said. Why didn't I do it?

My instant answer, most insufficient really, was: "Loyalty." What I meant, of course, was that the whole decision was something very personal to Matthew; involving, that's to say, not merely whatever outward consequences flowed from it, but involving his whole personality and the point of growth it has reached. It's a test—a test of his whole character and the possibility, which he has expressed a vague hope for, of "change". What he has really been meaning, underneath the explicit search for a change of outward circumstances, was really a change of character. I don't think I'm being pompous over this. I think that's what's really going on.

But, of course, it's impossible to explain this to the Adrians, and my attempt simply exasperated him. I had remarked that I had never seen Matthew really up against it before, implying, I suppose, that there was a certain fascination in seeing it now.

"And I hope to God you don't again," Adrian said.

"No, once is enough," I agreed.

"Once is too much, ducky," Adrian squeaked. To a client, of course, the whole object of life is to protect the patron from anything serious at all.

"Once may be just the right amount," I couldn't resist saying which, of course, infuriated him even more.

"You are encouraging him. I knew you were. I've warned him against you."

Nor can Grace see the problem in anything like the perspective that I think I see it in.

Naturally her close involvement and the danger to her own position obscure her judgement, while her very shallow psychologising produces for her all sorts of pat and easy answers. I'm not against psychiatry and the psycho-analysts, but I'm by no means sure that the popularisation of immensely complex notions hasn't done infinite harm. It's so easy to produce a slick solution nowadays, convincing on the surface but leaving out all the subtleties that matter. But I must admit I wasn't very good at explaining what I really meant.

We were discussing it the other night, Adrian, Grace and I; and I suggested—thinking Grace with all her theories would see this—that subconsciously there was a kind of way in which Matthew wants to be shown up. Indignant denials from both of them. What could I mean? Didn't they see, I said, that if the worst happened, he would simply have to "change"?

But even Grace couldn't see it. "But why should he want to change? Hasn't he got everything he wants?"

Curious that even now she should really think this. But she does. For she added, "He's got the best of both worlds. Isn't that good enough for anybody?"

155

And they refused to see it when I said that wasn't what it seemed like to him. And, pressed, I went on to suggest that he felt trapped. Grace—and, of course, one sees why—was very indignant.

"Trapped? I've given him absolute freedom. Too much, I dare say."

"Not trapped by you," I tried to explain, "but by life. It's his own fault entirely; and he recognises that. But he doesn't know how to escape. This—in a disastrous sort of way, admittedly—gives him an 'out'."

Grace had no patience with this, although I had thought it might be just along her lines.

"I don't know what you're getting at," she said very crossly. "What I do know is that he has responsibilities. To me. To Luke. To himself, and it's time he faced them."

This seemed to me a quite dotty view. An absurd refusal to accept Matthew as he is. "He isn't the slightest interested in his responsibilities," I insisted. "Never has been, never will be. Just the opposite. They're just what's partly driving him to this."

You might think that Grace would have accepted that at least by now. But no. "And you'ld just pander to that!"

Not at all, I said, I simply accepted it. Why couldn't they? It wasn't very admirable, perhaps. But Matthew had never set out to be admirable. He was what he was—a talent and nothing else really, and it was the talent he was trying to rescue. Because his life had been hostile to his talent. Surely they could both see that?

But neither could; they just defended his life as it is, and Grace wound up with her psychologising.

"What he needs now is being made to face the realities. That's what he's never done. It's simply adolescent to refuse to face the truth. I know. I'm used to dealing with adolescents and they do it all the time. He's just avoiding the issue as they all do. I'm going to face him with it absolutely squarely, so that he can't wriggle out of it. That's the only way to treat people like him."

And she brushed aside all my protestations. For at heart, of course, she is only an ordinary, rather simple woman, putting into more up-to-date phrases the sort of point of view tough governesses used to have. But she doesn't really see. She doesn't see that Matthew's talent hasn't really been working for some years, and if his talent isn't working he's a kind of stopped clock.

One mustn't forget, on the other hand, how much she has had to put up with. And she's done remarkably well, really. She's managed to make a substitute life for herself, centred largely round welfare work with adolescents. And it is perfectly true that if Matthew is exposed in public, she's going to look rather foolish in those circles—or anyhow it will obviously be very humiliating for her. But it is in the deepest sense, partly at any rate, her own fault; I don't say she's been a mere flatterer in the Adrian sense. But she has been much too content with the seeming success of Sir Matthew Prior, and the reflected glory of it, without applying her new-found knowledge to Matthew's real situation.

Poor Grace. And she was in a great state today when Matthew got Adrian to phone her and tell her he wasn't going to have her in court at all and didn't want her called. She came up in a flurry and I gather they had a real set-to.

[Matthew and Grace in the Albany flat]

"IT's sweet of you to have come, dear. But I wanted to save you the journey."

"I don't want to be saved anything. I want to help."

"I knew you would, but you can't. No one can."

"I've talked to Cruddle and he says Quick wants me in court. He says it will be a great point in your favour. He says that if I testify...."

"Look. I don't see how I can possibly take their advice. I really don't."

"But it's absurd. What's the good of engaging expensive counsel and not taking their advice?"

"You won't understand. But the conditions I'm offered are totally unacceptable."

"I should have thought any conditions were worth it to avoid a public disgrace."

"Not this one."

"Do you know or don't you where Luke got the drug from?"

"As it happens I do."

159

"Well, why haven't you told them already? Don't you want it all cleared up?"

"It doesn't seem to me quite so simple as that. Whose side am I supposed to be on?"

"You're on the side of stopping this horrible thing as best you can: that's being on Luke's side—in the long run."

"I'm not so sure. What about the short run, anyhow? What's Luke going to think of me, when he finds out I've given his pal away?"

"He needn't find out."

"One is always found out. As I've now discovered."

"Besides, to talk of it in those terms is nonsense. You're defending Luke from himself."

"I wouldn't want anyone—not anyone—taking that line over me. Do you think I could bear it if you or Luke informed on me to save me from myself? He's a right to his own secrets."

"Even if they're destroying him?"

"Even if they're destroying him. We've all a right to our own secrets, even the shabbiest of them, as long as we think we can keep them. When we fail—then God knows."

"But if you tell them what they want to know, you will keep your secrets?"

"Yes, at the expense of his."

"They'll find out anyway."

"That's not the point. I'm asked to turn informer."

"I can't think why you hesitate. It wouldn't harm Luke."

"I'm sure you can't Grace. What you don't understand is that this has really nothing to do with Luke. It's only incidental that he's involved, too. There are things one can do and there are things one can't. I don't see how I can do this. I'm all sorts of a shit, but I'm not an informer, am I?"

"Considering some of the things you do do. . . ."

"Now Grace that isn't very nice. And it's not like you."

"All right, I'm sorry for that. But how can I make you see sense? You don't want to be publicly exposed, do you? And me and Luke? All of us?"

"If I could possibly avoid it, do you think that I wouldn't? But look at it my way. Can you really see me going to the police and saying: it was young so-and-so who got Luke those drugs, and then seeing wretched young so-and-so being searched, arrested and probably carted off to prison, and knowing I was responsible?"

"But if he's trafficking in those horrible drugs he ought to be in prison!"

"In that case so ought I! . . . Oh, it's no use, Grace. You'll never see it. The trouble is you're a nice, uncomplicated, loyal character, without any temptations that I can see. If I'd been somebody I never was, you'd have been a happy woman, a proud wife, a good mother. You have all the virtues on your side. Life's been most unfair to you. Why should you suffer for my follies? There's no justice, is there? It's not much good saying I'm sorry. I'm not sorry for anything I've done. I'm just sorry to have landed you in it. But there it is! Innocence is no protection. You ought to have divorced me years ago. I've offered you the chance often enough."

"I thought of Luke."

"That hasn't done much good, has it? And now where's your plan for making a happy home for him? It was never much of a plan, if you ask me. Whatever damage there is was already done. But now, with a public scandal hanging over me, that's out, anyhow."

"And what about me? Have you thought of the effect of a public scandal on me?"

N5

"Yes, of course, there's that. What can I say, except that you've made your choice and you must take the consequences?"

"That wasn't very nice, either."

"No, it wasn't. I apologise. But about this I'm adamant. We can't really foretell the consequences of any of our actions. Perhaps if I told them what they want to know it would make no difference at all. Very likely not. All I can do at this point is trust my own feelings, and I feel that if I told them it would be despicable."

"Your feelings indeed! Your feelings! What feelings have you ever had except purely selfish feelings? Totally, absolutely ego-centred. Luke's in danger of becoming an addict. I'm in danger of being made to look in public the fool I've been made to look in private all these years. And all you think about is your precious feelings! What evidence have you for thinking your feelings are any guide to conduct, I'd like to know?"

"Of course, you're right. You're always right. It's one of the most annoying things about you. But the fact remains. I have to live with my feelings—such as they are."

"Live? Live where? After you've publicly exposed yourself?"

"A good question. I wish I knew the answer."

"You'll have to cancel your production. That's certain."

"Thank God for that! No. That's the least of my worries. Will you believe me if I say that you're not? And I'm going to keep you out of this as far as I can. You take my advice and wash your hands of me. I've been no good to you for years. Forget all about me. We'll make the break complete."

"Do you really think that I'll desert you now, just when you most need help?"

"I don't want help, *your* help anyhow. You've done more than your share. Get out, my dear, while the going's bad. It'll only make matters worse if I have to worry about you too, and the effect on you. Spare me that. I'm not involving anyone else, you, Luke or anyone. It's time I faced things for myself, and I'd rather face them on my own and make my decision for myself alone."

"But surely . . ."

"Please. Please. Just cut off. It's sweet of you to have come. I knew you would. But you can't help. You can only make things worse. Believe me, all I want now is to be left to face this thing my own way. I must and you must let me. If you really want to be helpful, I promise you that's the only way you can."

"You're stubborn, Matthew. You always were. You think of nothing but yourself. All these years I've made my own life. I've had to. And even that you're prepared to destroy. You may be able to face the world. Your world, anyhow. I shan't be able to face mine. It takes some facing as it is. The absentee husband. I've explained that as best I could. But how explain this? Goodness knows I've done my best to understand. But I can't expect others to. I have some knowledge of these things. They haven't."

"You've been wonderful, Grace, and I've behaved abominably. What else can I say? If I could possibly spare you this humiliation I would. But how can I persuade you that I can't? I just couldn't bring myself to do it. They asked me before—before all this happened—and I wouldn't then. What sort of shit would I look to myself if I did it now just to save my own skin?"

"I suppose it's no good arguing with you. What's the good? I see I don't count any more. Even a little wasp like Adrian counts for more than I do."

[Matthew in his dressing-room with Stephen]

"No, it's no good you all trying to persuade me
to take their advice, because I won't do it. I
know it's sensible, I know it's reasonable. I
know it's practicable. But all the same I won't.
I couldn't live with myself if I did. It's as
simple as that. They argue that it's either Luke
or me, or, alternatively, as the lawyers say, he'd
never find out. But that isn't the point."

"Are you absolutely sure?"

"The point is *I* should know. I'm not thinking of Luke so much. That's what I can't make
you all see. I may have compromised with
society. Got away with a reputation for
respectability—actor, father, knight. God knows
it was a mistake, but at least I knew more or
less what I was doing. But when it comes to
more than compromise—to coming down on
their side, to joining them because I can't beat
them, no, there I stick. It may seem idiotic, I
don't care. I couldn't do it. That's all. Here I
stick. I'm all kinds of a shit but I'm not that
kind of a shit. I don't inform."

166

"You realise just what that means, if you really do stick to it?"

"I become an outsider. Which is what I always ought to have been anyhow. And I become it by choice. . . . It's rather maddening that it won't look like choice; more like being cast off. But there it is. That's the price I must pay for my conformity. If only I'd stuck out from the start I should now be a grizzled old rebel. I suppose grizzled old rebels *are* rather ridiculous figures at the best of times, but at least they're on solid ground. A cast-off hasn't much standing, has he?"

"Not much. And that's why you've got to be very sure what you're doing."

"Why did I ever take that damned knighthood. That was the greatest mistake. And it's not just a question of the higher the pinnacle, the greater the fall. Though there is that. But it was such a senseless piece of petty vanity. The others all had one, why not me? And then, I suppose, in my heart of hearts I knew I wasn't really using my gift and the knighthood was a sort of salve. But fancy me tricking myself like that! How low can one creep? Did I really fancy it would make up for the lack of character? Because, you see, I'm not entirely disposed

to accept our easy explanation of my failure—
to give it its true name. Yes, failure, let's face it.
It's so easy to attribute it all to the changed
conditions, the shift of fashion in the theatre,
the social revolution, the new generation.
Doesn't that absolve me all too easily?"

"I don't know about that."

"I do! I belong to an older—and let's make
no bones about it—a better tradition. Grant the
revolution of fashion all its virtues, and it's all
the same not permanent or immutable. And
that needed saying and it needed demon-
strating. Couldn't I have done that, or tried,
even if I'd failed? And why didn't I? Precisely
for the reason that's at the root of all my
troubles. Standing against the tide is a sign of
one's age. I wasn't going to admit I was the age
I was. I had to be on the side of the young. I
wasn't going to be thought an old square.

"So as the new movement arrived, there I
was applauding it and cheering it on. Giving
interviews about how clever the young men
were, courting them, asking them to parties,
and even—Christ fuck it!—half concurring in
their assumption that my kind of theatre was
dead. Castrating myself to gain their regard. It
stinks. I've never really admitted it before, but

that's what I did—gave up, really, and just pottered along, accepting knighthoods and trying to be with-it at the same time.

"I even tried a few of their misbegotten, ill-written, graceless plays, so help me! Just to be with-it. And of course, they were disastrous. I've only one line, and that's style, and without it behind me I'm sunk. My vocal chords vibrate rightly and instantly to style. And my vocal chords are right and I know they're right."

"Bravo!"

"And I ought never to have abandoned the conviction—or even tried to, for, after all, what is art about if not style? And the more style-less life becomes the greater the need to remind ourselves that we humans have in our time lived with style and died—good God—with style, and will have to learn to do so again. To die in style, certainly, for, Christ, how badly we die nowadays! Kept alive too long and shuffling out of life without so much as a decent gesture between us! That's what Tragedy is about in my view. It's not the meaning of the human condition or whatever. It's about dying, and dying with dignity and dying with style. And I don't mind boasting I can die better than any of them.

"And if Tragedy is about dying with style, isn't Comedy about living with style? And that doesn't, of course, just mean the 'nice conduct of a clouded cane'—it's a question of form and panache and carrying life off with wit. You're quite right, I could have taught them a thing or two about that, if they'd let me. But they wouldn't listen, I supposed. Or that, anyhow, was my excuse. It won't wash, of course. I could have made them listen. I could at least have tried. And now it's too late.

"Well, I shall need every bit of style I can muster in the next few days. The only trouble is that life and art aren't the same thing. I can act with style, I know. But whether I can live with style is another matter altogether. We shall see all too soon."

PART
THREE

ACTOR FOOLS POLICE
Plea for legalisation of marijuana

CHARGED today with driving under the influence of drugs and drink and illegal possession of cannabis, Sir Matthew Prior, 58, the well-known actor, admitted he had played a prank on the police.

He was dressed up for a female impersonation at a party he was going to when he had the accident which led to his arrest. Apologising to the court for a joke which "turned out to be less funny than he thought at the time", Sir Matthew explained that the policeman on the beat and the sergeant at the desk had both taken him for a "real" woman. "I allowed myself to be flattered by the success of my impersonation," he told the magistrate, "and didn't tell them who I really was."

The magistrate (Mr Eric Robertson) dismissed this aspect of the case as "a red herring". The serious thing was that Sir Matthew had not only admitted being under the influence of drugs, and having drugs in his possession, but had tried to justify the crime.

Sir Matthew made an impassioned plea from the box for the legalisation of marijuana. It was no worse, he asserted, than alcohol or cigarettes: in fact, it was probably less addictive than either. If the police were freed from the duty of pursuing the comparatively innocent smokes of "pot", they could use their resources more effectively to clamp down on the really dangerous things, the hard drugs.

173

Interrupting him, the magistrate said that Sir Matthew was doing himself no good by adding defiance to wrong-doing. The law was the law and Sir Matthew was deliberately flouting it. If he continued to do so, he would be sent to prison. Meanwhile he would fine him a total of £500 on all the charges.

[From Stephen Luther's diary]

WELL, well, well. It hasn't turned out as badly
as we feared after all. In fact, to judge by the
headlines, Matthew has come out of it pretty
well. Most of them treat the dressing up as a
joke, a successful joke against the police. And
several others headline his plea for the legalisation of "pot". ACTOR DEFENDS THE YOUNG.
That kind of thing. Of course, those who are
"in the know" will know, but what does that in
fact amount to? A couple of dozen people
within the theatre world, and a handful of
Fleet Street gossip columnists. They may yet
use the occasion for some snide remarks, but I
don't think that will damage Matthew. I think
we can say that he's got off really scot free.

This was, of course, largely due to the magistrate and, to give him his due, to Quick, who
was very prompt in getting that whole business
out of the way. But we had some nasty moments. The morning started badly with a
blazing row between Matthew and Quick when
Quick discovered that Matthew had absolutely

175

put his foot down about Grace attending. And then again, Matthew had rather hurt their professional pride by refusing to accept their mitigation plea.

The nasty moment was, of course, when the prosecuting counsel, who was leading the first constable through his evidence, blandly said, "I suppose you know Sir Matthew by appearance fairly well. Did you recognise him at once?" And when the constable said "No", he was asked even more blandly, "Ah, why was that?" Sensation in court, as they say, at the constable's reply. The reporters' pencils fairly flew over the paper. The magistrate blinked and started up and requested the explanation to be repeated. But Quick was very smart up on his feet and no less smooth and bland. Very deferentially he asked if his client might be allowed to make an explanation and an apology at this point and, the magistrate agreeing, he led Matthew convincingly through his story. Matthew was excellent at this point, too, and between them they got the magistrate on their side over it. Or perhaps it was simply that the magistrate didn't see the complications and wanted to get on with the real business.

In any case when the prosecution, as Butcher

had prophesied, tried to push it with "In that case, Sir Matthew, why didn't you give that explanation to the constable, or at least to the desk sergeant?", old Robertson brushed the question aside. "All this seems to me a red herring," he said. "The charges against Sir Matthew are extremely serious. I don't want them glossed over as if they were part of some university prank. All I will say about that is that I hope you realise, Sir Matthew, the sort of folly that taking this noxious drug can lead you into. Now then, will the prosecution address itself to the charges before the court?"

And no more was heard of the impersonation. With that out of the way so successfully, Quick evidently thought Matthew might have had a change of heart, and framed his questions so as to give him the chance to avail himself of the defence they had worked out.

"This was the first occasion, wasn't it, Sir Matthew, that you had ever smoked marijuana?"

And when Matthew said, "Yes"—

"Will you tell the court why you decided to experiment on this occasion?"

But Matthew wasn't having any. "I wanted to see for myself what it was like."

Quick evidently took this for a cue: "For yourself, yes. I'm right in saying, aren't I, that your son is up on a similar charge. Had that something to do with your decision?"

Matthew turned him down flat.

"Nothing whatever. Why should it have? There's a lot of talk about drugs. I simply wanted to make up my own mind about it."

This brought old Robertson in. He'd been looking rather puzzled by the way things were going.

"Do you realise now that that was a very irresponsible thing to do?"

But Matthew turned him down, too.

"I'm afraid I don't think so. We all drink and smoke, which are no less drugs than this. In fact some people say this does less harm."

Robertson got sterner. "It led you to take out your motor-car when you were in no fit state to drive, and it's only your good luck that the accident which ensued wasn't much more serious."

But Matthew, having evidently recovered his nerve completely, was quite determined to say exactly where he stood and read us all this lecture—compounded of those articles and letters in *The Times*—about the comparative harmlessness of marijuana, how it ought to be legalised, thus setting the police free for the more serious business, etc., till old Robertson interrupted him with: "Thank you for your lecture, Sir Matthew, but let me remind you that the law is the law and you won't do your case any good by adding defiance to wrong-doing."

And then he asked Quick if he had anything more to say, and Quick couldn't do anything but ask for the indulgence of the court, which he didn't get. Robertson weighed in with the usual—"this grave social menace", "thorough irresponsibility", "disgraceful example to the young", and ended up by saying that Matthew could count himself lucky not to have been sent to prison. But if there was any recurrence of the offence, he certainly would be, and the £500 fine, and that was that.

We all felt that he had got off pretty lightly as we came out of court. But we weren't at all certain how lightly until we got the first evening papers. It was all rather like a first night. How would the notices go? Well, as I said, they were surprisingly favourable, almost on Matthew's side, and we celebrated, if rather gingerly, in the evening. Matthew wouldn't go out. He felt that a lot of them would be looking at him all too knowingly. But hundreds of people rang up and congratulated him and he went to bed pretty contented, and was reassured again by the morning papers.

[Matthew with Stephen at the Albany flat]

"No, of course I didn't want to be a martyr, why should I? But isn't that anyhow what in a sort of way I've become? Look at the cuttings! 'Actor defends marijuana.' 'Is hemp worse than whisky?' 'Knight stands up for the young.' My squalid little episode turns me into a sort of crusader for youth.

"As for Grace. Well, I asked for it and I got it. And she's right to try and save herself; it's what we've all got to do. How Luke will react, goodness only knows. . . . Yes, I admit it was an anti-climax, like the whole of my life. I'm the classic case, aren't I? Youth, beauty and talent. Gobbling up success as if it were mine by right. And never facing the fact that youth passes and beauty fades. Perhaps they weren't so unlucky after all, those romantic characters pegging out young! Imagine Keats doddering on into a Wordsworthian old age. Rimbaud settling down in a French provincial town to raise a family of ungrateful provincial brats.

"Or would they have been content to remain

provincial brats? That's a thought! I wouldn't have. Somehow or other, wouldn't I have got hold of the whole story of my father, so carefully concealed from me by my reformed papa and bourgeoise mother? Wouldn't I have made my way to Paris, and traced the whole course of the relationship with Verlaine and discovered the daemonic poems and opened for myself a whole new world? ... And would my Luke have taken a different view of me if I hadn't gone all respectable and covered up my tracks so carefully, if he knew about you and me, and the nights in the Café Liégois and the fetishist parties?"

"Well, now I suppose he does know."

"I wonder. What does he know or what doesn't he? 'Actor fools police.' Won't he prefer to believe that? He's bound to have heard rumours. . . . But one only half believes them about one's own parents. There they are. Up above one. Respectable, respected figures. One doesn't so easily believe that they still aren't. I never really believed that my father, a middle-class stockbroker, was having it off with the typist. But he was. . . . What do *I* seem in spite of what he hears? Not what I am, that's for sure. Not an ageing star grasping at his last memories of youth, struggling against facing what he has become. No, in spite of the rumours, I guess, I'm still for him the establishment figure. The Sir Matthew that attends the garden parties with Lady Prior on his arm. The Sir Matthew of the first night photographs and the charity matinées.

"Well, it's about time he grew up and faced the truth, the truth about me, what I really am. I'm going to face him with it now, have it right out in the open and see how he likes it. I'm tired of pretending—pretending with everybody, with him, with the world, with the public. Yes, I admit it, I half wanted the truth to come out there and then all over the papers. There it would have been for everyone to see. Yes, one day, I think I'm going to have a show-down with that young man. My last gesture before I go. . . .

"Go? What am I talking about, go? I haven't got to go. You were quite right, Stephen, though I denied it. What I was doing, half the time, unconsciously, I suppose, was forcing my own hand too. I wasn't courting disaster: I was courting decision."

"Yes, I see that."

"Very well, then. Have the last few horrible

days taught me anything? Have I learned my lesson? Or am I simply going to relapse? No, no. Not that. Let's talk of that idea of yours. I hardly took it in before. Let's work on it. See if there's really anything in it. If it's not that, I don't know what it is.

"You see I wasn't, I realise, being only stupidly trendy in admiring the young. Not in every way. They've done some splendid pieces of bashing. Bashing the old class nonsense, for instance, that disastrous English thing. I'm with them there, and, don't you see, by becoming Sir Matthew I stepped half into just that world. You've your place in the hierarchy. You can do this and not that, think this and not that. And there's no getting away from it. You're placed, classified, docketed. Sir Matthew, with all that means to the English middle-class mind. The Hampshire house, Lady Prior, opening the village fair. Entertaining the neighbours and listening to their fatuous views on bringing back the cat and sterilising the queers and getting rid of the blacks. I've got to get away from all that. And then, when I have, then I shall be alone with my gift, my talent. . . . I haven't always used it well. When I was young I was often content with the easy and the shallow, as we all were in those days. But I more than most. It didn't seem to matter. There was so much time. Time for anything and everything. But as the years close in and I'm ready at last to use it properly, nobody wants to know. Not here, anyway, not at the moment.

"So let's get down to it seriously and soberly, hammer something out. We must have a theatre, too, that's essential. We could make it in the end something like Glyndebourne was in the early days—absolute perfection. Thank God I've got the lolly for it—and if it were a success there'll be all those Foundations to supply more.

"We must make it work. I must earn my distinction once again. And I could. Now. *Me.* This me, with my special gift to give it authority, at my age to give it weight. Yes, at last I shall find my age on my side. Not just having to face it—positively using it.

'Grow old along with me!
The best is yet to be!'

Perhaps that blithe old optimist was right after all.

"So we'll get down to it together. Get out

sketches, plans, think up ideas. Go out and
survey the ground. For I'm not going back, not
after this, not to the half life. I may be fifty-
eight. I am what I've become. All right, I admit
it. I face it. I look it straight in the eyes, in the
liver spots, in the wrinkles, and I say to it,
'You're not done yet, my boy!' I may have been
let off—I have been—but let me take advantage
of what I faced when I thought I wasn't going
to be."

TODAY Grace walked out on us, and I must admit it was done with great dignity. She was really rather splendid. We were gathered in the flat mulling over the whole incident and talking desultorily about the future. There was Adrian and Grace and me. Matthew didn't join us— he was lying down, Adrian reported, with a codeine and a whisky. As Grace had come up especially "to talk things over", she was naturally rather hipped. Adrian was rather jubilant, the morning papers also having treated Matthew very well.

"He's going to come out of it very well and there won't be an empty seat in the house, my dears," and so on.

Presently Grace looked at her watch, got up and announced she was going to catch a train.

"But you haven't seen Matty yet," Adrian wailed.

"No," she said. "If he can't be bothered to come out and see me, I don't see why I should be bothered to hang about."

187

I tried to put in a soothing word, suggesting Matthew had been under a great strain.

"And do you think I haven't been under a great strain too?" she said, quite quietly and firmly. "Do you know what it's been like sitting here on tenterhooks waiting to know whether one's husband is going to be exposed all over the papers?"

I saw she was working herself up and urged Adrian to go and get Matthew in. But she said, "No, I don't want to see him, to tell you the truth."

"Oh, come on, ducks," Adrian pleaded. "You know our Matty!"

And then she let fly:

"Yes, I know 'our' Matty. We all know our Matty. We've all devoted ourselves for years to our Matty. We've listened for hour after hour. We've rallied round in the moments of crisis and poured out congratulations in the hours of success. We've adapted ourselves to his moods, forgiven him his slights, pretended not to notice his indifference, and come back again for more. And what have we got out of it in return? Precisely nothing."

I suggested that we were all exhausted and

had much better meet again in a day or two when we'd recovered. But Grace wasn't having it.

"No," she said, "I've had enough. I'ld have stood by him, I suppose, if the worst had happened. But I've been let off, too. I've had enough. I'm not going through all that again for anybody. He's wanted a break. Well, now he's got one. He's talked of a divorce. Now he can have one. I've had enough."

It didn't seem like mere hysteria. I was convinced, then, that she really meant it, though Adrian tried to go on cooling her down. She was, anyhow, surprisingly calm and decisive.

"You can tell him from me," she said "that I'm finished, it's all washed up. I'm not being hysterical. I'm not blackmailing him. I've just come to a conclusion. Rather obvious. Rather simple."

"What's that, ducks?" Adrian asked.

And she had found for herself a splendid exit line. From the door, looking round at us both with her chin up, she said:

"It's that I don't really even like him very much any more!"

DARLING JOANIE,

Have you seen the news? Extraordinary, isn't it? What do you make of it? What is he up to now? No one gave me any warning, of course. I was just left to read it in the evening papers like anyone else! You can imagine the shock! At first I thought, well, really, who would have thought the old man to have had so much blood in him? I was almost admiring him. And it really was rather splendid the way he fooled the fuzz. I had a good laugh over that.

But as I read them again and again I began to see the idea. You see how well he comes out of it? The square defending the young. Oh, they're a cunning lot of bastards. I can just see them working it all out, can't you? Picking the line of defence that will reflect the greatest credit on him and fuck everyone else?

And, of course, they all stand up for one another. The Old Boys' network with emphasis on the Old. I'm caught just transporting the stuff, and it's the wicked young with their depraved habits. He's caught driving under the influence and it's "Famous Actor Defends the Young". Getting it every possible way. Trust them!

But all the same, I do wonder how long he's been at it, and when he started. . . . I long to find out. Perhaps Adrian will give him away. He loves a bit of gossip. Of course, I've known for ages that he was queer, anyhow when he was young. You couldn't keep a thing like that quiet in the theatre world. And who's caring, anyway? In fact he might even have been quite fun to have met years ago. What happens to people as they get old? Do they have to get all respectable? Shall I do it too, do you think? You know, the country house, the well-cut tweeds, the modest success, the perfect example of the exemplary knight, with his wife and his family and his clubs?

Do you think that pot is what he's been at all the time, though? Does that explain why he's gone all soft round the edges? Why he hasn't done anything decent for goodness knows how many years? Why he's quite content to go on repeating the successes of his youth without ever changing or experimenting or showing any courage at all?

Perhaps I shall have to learn to be charitable and forgive him if it's the pot that's been doing it. Because, of course, that's one of the things I've never been able to forgive him for, for being one of those that's held the theatre back thirty years. What else is this series of one-man recitals, bringing out again all those silver notes and tremolos that they adored thirty years ago?

I've thought of something very funny. Do you think it my duty as a good son to ride in and rescue him from his depraved habits, and then, renouncing his drug, he might come off that old muck and move on somewhere creative? It would be a rather marvellous reversal, wouldn't it? Me being his salvation? Do you know, even quite seriously, it's quite an idea? He must have had something in the old days, mustn't he? And if he has been indulging all this time, it would have taken the edge off him. It does, you know, makes you complacent. That's why, in fact, after the first few times, I gave it up completely. I didn't want to end up like him! But, of course, I didn't realise that that's what it was with him. It does fit, doesn't it? I wonder what sort of reception I'd get if I tried. Well, it couldn't be worse, could it? And it would be rather comic. The indulgent son welcoming back into the fold the prodigal father! I really think I'll have a bash. Just for the giggle. It wouldn't work, I'm sure, but it wouldn't do any harm.

Of course, it all depends on quite what happens when my case comes up. But if I had to go to prison, it would make the comic reversal even more stupendous! My case comes up the day after tomorrow. When it's over, I'll see. I might really try an approach.

Must dash off now. See you at the weekend, and let me know what you think.

Your own

LUKE

[*From a daily paper*]

YOUNG ACTOR CONDITIONALLY
DISCHARGED ON DRUGS CHARGE
Evil Influence of his Elders

WHEN Luke Prior, 20, actor, came up at Bow
Street on remand yesterday on a charge of
being in illegal possession of cannabis to the
value of £125, the magistrate, Mr Eric
Robertson, gave him a conditional discharge.

Refusing the police request for a further
remand, Mr Robertson said that much more
was now known about the case. Since Prior was
last up before him, his own father, Sir
Matthew Prior, the actor, had also been tried
on a charge of possessing drugs, and had
pleaded guilty. Addressing Prior, the magistrate said: "I have more sympathy with you
now than I had when you last came up before
me. If your elders, and what should be your
betters, themselves indulge in this noxious
habit, it is not entirely surprising that you
should have imitated them. I warn you most
seriously against doing so, and I urge you to
disregard your father's spurious and inaccurate
defence of this habit. Apart from anything else
it is strictly against the law, and if you're
found guilty of it again you will go to prison."

IT was wonderfully funny when Matthew announced our plan to Adrian. Adrian had come round after fixing up the meeting Matthew wanted with Luke. Matthew said, all right, he'd see him the last thing before he went, for we were off on a new jag.

"What's all this about, then?" Adrian asked suspiciously.

And Matthew said just that we were going out of England to Marrakech, California, Australia. We hadn't decided which.

"And become two old hippies in flower clothes with bells on?" Adrian, quite wittily in his fashion, suggested.

So Matthew told him about the Actor's Studio and our own theatre and doing exactly what we wanted.

"Better make it Marrakech, then," Adrian suggested in the same vein. But he obviously deeply disliked the idea and distrusted me. Asked what he thought, when Matthew had finished, he finally came out with:

"Rather you than me, that's what I think," and, pressed for a reason, said it sounded too arty for him. But then gave what I take to be his real reason:

"Not very glamorous, is it, either?"

"And what a relief that will be," Matthew said. "All the ballyhoo will go and lots of idiotic things with it," and he developed one of his tirades:

"No more deferring to the young; no more praising the half-baked; no more reading in the Sunday papers the latest pimply young author of his first play being solemnly interviewed by Ken Tynan. No more coloured supplement pictures of Luke and the other overnight young stars flaunting the latest gear and clutching the latest dollies. No more notices telling us how old-hat we are compared with you-know-who. No more lectures from Charles Marowitz on Total Theatre and After. No more 'happenings' and actor's antics and audience participation and producer's field days. No more fusty Central European symbolism translated by Martin Esslin."

Later I had a real ding-dong with Adrian over it, and I don't make the mistake of underestimating Adrian. Whatever he is, he's no fool. His point was that Matthew simply wasn't the kind of person to do this sort of thing. "Maybe he could have been in the early days when you knew him best, but he certainly isn't now. He never thinks of anything for himself. It's all done for him."

What I couldn't make Adrian see is that I'm doing all the organising and arranging. With his very limited view of the world—confined really to the narrowest of theatrical horizons—he can't know, of course, that running a large university department, and in the special circumstances of a "developing" country, has given me a very wide administrative experience and grasp. Matthew still won't have to "think of anything for himself", either. He'll still be very much a star, coming in to give the place its cachet and its character and, of course, I know him well enough to know that he must be treated, protected, cossetted, if you like, though he is—or anyhow used to be and surely that hasn't been lost—much shrewder over material things than his manner would suggest.

Of course I don't know how it will work out. I shall do my best to make it a great success, and in my vision of it a whole exciting new development might take place, if we were, say, in Australia or California, where the theatre is thin on the ground. It will depend also, of course, on getting just the right people round us, people with ideas who will complement Matthew's own gifts.

I don't burke the fact that it may be an illusion on my part, and may turn out a dismal failure. But if it does, nothing's lost except money which he can afford and time which he now needs—needs, I mean, to get over the present hump. Adrian's view was, in his nature, even more cynical.

"You know how you two will end up, if you try to carry this through?" he finally said.

"That we shall have to see," I said, "shan't we?"

"You'll end up," he said, with immense relish, "the pair of you, ageing queens in the African bars, talking about something that never comes off."

I suppose he's right. I suppose there's a risk of that, too, though it would surprise me if that's where I ended up.

Finally Adrian blustered: "I don't believe he's serious, anyhow."

And I had an answer for that. "Go round in

front tonight, then, and see if that will convince you!"

He did look a bit startled at that and demanded what I meant. But I wasn't going to spoil Matthew's *coup de foudre*.

"Just you go and see," I said.

[*Matthew in his dressing-room with his son, Luke*]

"So you've come?"

"Weren't you expecting me?"

"Adrian told me you'ld be along. But I wasn't so sure."

"Why not, then?"

"You make a habit of not turning up when you're supposed to."

"Well, I've turned up this time, haven't I? Would you rather I hadn't?"

"No, come in, sit down. Have a drink. . . . How are things? How's Mary? No, it's Joan now, isn't it?"

"Yes."

"Have I met her?"

"No, I don't think you have. She's in rep in Nottingham."

"Good?"

"*I* think so. . . ."

"Have you got anything else coming up?"

"Another film."

"Lucky you!"

"Yes."

"Good part?"

"It's the lead, really."

"Fine. When do you start?"

"Next week. . . ."

"No trouble over your case—or mine for that matter!"

"Not that I've heard; I shouldn't think so with this set-up."

"You were discharged?"

"Yes. Thanks to you."

"Is that what you came along to say?"

"Yes, sort of. Though you might have warned me—about you, I mean. I only knew about it when I saw it in the headlines."

"We weren't exactly in communication, were we? But don't believe all you read in the papers. They made me out a sort of crusader. It wasn't like that in court, I can tell you. The beak gets the last word and you can be sure he didn't fail to put the boot in. I was chopped up proper. . . ."

"There is one thing I'd rather like to know."

"What's that?"

"It's a bit difficult . . . but how long have you been on it? The hemp, I mean."

"Oh, that. Why do you ask?"

"I've been thinking. It might explain some things."

"Like what?"

"Well . . ."

"A sort of all round degeneration, do you mean?"

"No, not that. But it does impair the judgement a bit."

"Is that your experience?"

"I don't use it now. But from what I've seen . . ."

"And you came round to give Dad a warning—or a helping hand to get him off it?"

"Not exactly, no, but I do understand about it."

"Well, dammit, you damned little prig. How you dare!"

"Evidently my mistake."

"Entirely your mistake. I did take it, if you want to know, just that once to see what you got out of it."

"But you denied that in the box."

"I didn't think you'ld thank me for using you as an excuse. Quick worked out a perfect defence along those lines and it would have answered, too."

"And you didn't use it because of me?"

"No, that's not it. If you want to know the truth, I wasn't thinking about you at all. I was simply thinking of myself."

"That doesn't surprise me."

"Now you're just playing for sympathy. Look here, let's get things straight. You think I'm in your way. Christ knows why. You're doing well enough on your own. You resent being my son. You resent whatever it's done to you, though it's done you nothing but good. O.K. though, I understand that. You want to have made it entirely on your own. And you're never quite sure whether you have. And you never will be sure. You'd better be clear about that. You are my son and there it is. You can like it or not. Lump it you must."

"More's the pity."

"Oh, for Christ's sake grow up, can't you? And get this clear. I resent you, too. I resent your success, I resent your youth, I resent your looks. I resent your making me feel old. Most, I resent your success. You haven't earned it. It's dropped into your lap. Do you know how bad you are? When I saw you in that Royal Court shindig I was ashamed of you. Your breath control is non-existent, your phrasing is vile, you've no technique at all. You haven't worked at it and you don't work at it. How much time do you put in at voice training? How often do you go to the gym?"

"I don't need to. . . . I'm quite . . ."

"Of course you need it, we all need it. Control of every muscle. You've practically none at all. You've got a pretty face and a pert personality and you just parade them. They won't last long, let me remind you—they won't see you far."

"They're not doing too badly."

"Yes, in films, where you don't do the work, the director does. He just uses the bits of you he wants. Take my advice, if you're going on as you are, stick to films. You won't be found out so easily there. You'll get away with it for quite a long time, given good directors. And you'll be a regular pop star, given enough idiotic girls. And that's about all you're good for, giving the girls a kick."

"So that's what you think of me?"

"When I do think of you."

"Well, that clears the air pretty thoroughly, doesn't it?"

"Doesn't it!"

"Shall I tell you what I think?"

"It's your turn, though I know what you're going to say."

"What then?"

"That it's time I gave up, that I'm all technique, and that that technique is old hat, anyhow. That I've had it. That they don't want to know, and they're quite right. Something like that?"

"No, what I was going to say was that if you care so little, why should you bother to resent me?"

"The old always resent the young. It's a law of nature. We resent it that you can still do it, when our powers are going off. We resent you thinking you know everything when we know you know nothing. I don't resent just you. I resent the lot of you. And while I'm about it, I'll tell you this, too. I'm not giving up. I'm not making way for you. My shoes aren't empty and I'll thank you not to try to step into them."

"O.K. O.K. You've made your point. But I think you might at least do one thing."

"Well?"

"Be your real age."

"And what exactly do you mean by that?"

"Why can't you settle down, you and mother, properly? And why can't you give up apeing the young? You can't compete on our terms, so why try? If you've got to go on having failure after failure in public, then I suppose you've got to. But why have you got to go on being in the swim all the time? Telling the papers how much you appreciate the young? Asking them to your parties, making up to them? Courting them? Trying to be with-it?"

"All that means as far as you're concerned, is that you want something to kick against. You want an old-fashioned Old Man for a father. One you can rebel against and show what a wild young thing you are. Well, you won't get it from me. I don't give a bugger how undisciplined you are, how late you are for your matinées, how sloppy you are at rehearsals. In my day you got the sack for that sort of thing, and so will anybody who tries it on me, however pretty and popular he is."

"You needn't go on. When I said you'd cleared the air, I really meant it. If you want to resent me, I can't stop you. But I shan't resent you any more. You've made it perfectly clear that I mean nothing in your life, so why should you mean anything in mine?"

"Fine. Fine, that's how I want it. I produced you and I launched you, for better or for worse.

But that's the end of it as far as I'm concerned. You think I'm finished. But I'm not. I've got my life to lead and I'm not going to lead it to suit you, let me tell you. I may seem old to you. But I don't seem old to myself. I haven't reached the settling down stage yet, and I'm not jumping that gun for your benefit. So don't count on it. I'm not settling down with your mother, I'm getting a divorce."

"If you do get one, I hope anyhow you will at least be more careful."

"Careful? What do you mean?"

"You say you were pretty lucky to get away with things in court the other day. We don't want any scandals, do we?"

"Because they might damage your image?"

"I've a right to look after that, haven't I?"

"Not at my expense, you haven't."

"At least perhaps next time you're in trouble, you'll warn me in advance?"

"And you think I might be?"

"I'm not absolutely innocent, you know. I can't help hearing things."

"About me?"

"About your . . . private life."

"And what have you heard?"

"You know as well as I do."

"But *how* well do you know. That's the point. Precisely?"

"I know you've always liked the boys. I know about Stephen and you in the past. Look, I don't mind. That's nothing to do with me. Some of my best friends are queer. But a scandal would be a . . . a pity."

"You'd better know everything, then, while you're about it. Perhaps you have as much right to know as I have to *be*. Because I warn you, I am what I am. If you're going to get a shock, and you very nearly did the other day when I was in court—you'd better know exactly what kind of a shock you're in for. At least you needn't be taken by surprise. There's another thing about your generation that you don't recognise—how lucky you are to have grown up in times when anything goes. And if anything goes there's no need, I suppose, to conceal anything. All the same there are things and things, aren't there? Did you believe what you read about my fooling the police?"

"Yes, that was rather fun, wasn't it?"

"Did you *believe* it? About going to a party where I was giving female impersonations?"

"Yes, I suppose I did."

"Have you ever seen me give female impersonations?"

"No, but I don't see why you shouldn't."

"Well, I don't. Not in that sense, I don't. But there's another sense in which I do. Go to that cupboard there. Not that one, the other . . . open it . . . what's there? Well, what do you see?"

"Dresses, jumpers, skirts, high-heeled shoes, wigs."

"Do you see?"

"Yes. I see."

"Now you know, if there is a scandal, what sort of a scandal you're in for. Or did you know that already? Had the rumour of this reached you, too?"

"I had heard something . . . someone had said . . . But I didn't think . . . I didn't quite realise . . ."

"Well, now you've got to realise. It's true. Something that has to be faced. . . . What are you thinking?"

"I don't know exactly . . . except perhaps . . . I'm sorry."

"Why should you be sorry?"

". . . It seems so sad."

"Sad?"

"Isn't it? Isn't it, I mean, to have to . . . not to be able not to. Even now?"

"At my age, you mean?"

"Yes, if you like."

"Give me a drink. A strong one. Help yourself. I think I see. Yes, I think I see now another reason, the strongest, why I've always resented you. You knowing makes me feel ashamed of myself. You always would have, I see now, once you found out. Up till now I wasn't ashamed, never! It was fun. I enjoyed it. It amused me. More, it gave me the biggest possible kick. . . . I was careful, of course, I had to be. When we were young, Stephen and me, we went abroad when the fit took me. Nearly always, anyhow."

"When you're young I do see, I do really. You know, I might, for a giggle. Well, I wouldn't, I suppose, but I might. But now. . . ."

"It's not something you grow out of. Not me, anyhow. And don't look at me like that. You're making me embarrassed."

"I don't mean to. I'm just sorry, like I said. So that's what you meant about last week's court and what I might have read?"

"I got away with it at the last moment. I was

let off. But I was sorry. I'd rather you'd read about it."

"I'd rather you told me. Much rather. I'm glad you have."

"Come to that, so am I, now."

"And you having told me . . . I shouldn't mind so much."

"Then I can tell you something else. In the future you won't have to know."

"You're giving it up?"

"It's no good promising that. I've given it up already, several times. But I still do it. I did last week. That damned hemp of yours. No, but I'm going away. Out of England."

"You are? Now? Why?"

"I've had enough of this. I'm starting again. An Actor's Studio. Stephen and I are going to get one going. Marrakech, California, perhaps Australia. Not here, anyhow. So if it does happen again, it's not likely to affect you."

"Don't think you have to . . . now I know . . . I wouldn't mind . . . I'd just grin."

"And bear it?"

"No . . . why? Who am I to disapprove?"

"Yes, that's one good thing about the new young. You're anyhow not censorious. But it isn't that. It's everything. It's my position, my marriage, my work in the theatre. They've all come to a stop. I'll tell you this, Luke, you couldn't despise this show I'm putting on now more than I do."

"The stuff they chose for you is rather feeble, isn't it?"

"Have you seen it then?"

"Yes, as a matter of fact I have."

"Surprise, surprise! It's lousy and I know it, and I'm more ashamed of it than I am of this. Ashamed that I could ever have agreed to do it. Well, I'm cutting away. I'll tell you all about it if it would amuse you."

"I'd like to hear; it sounds rather fascinating."

"O.K. Then do me a special favour, will you? Go round in front tonight? And after, I'll take you out to dinner."

"Tonight? It's a bit awkward tonight. . . ."

"I rather specially want you there tonight, it may surprise you."

"O.K. I'll be there. I'll just go and make a phone call."

"Off you go then. They'll give you a seat . . . and Luke!"

"Yes."

"You're O.K. really, aren't you?"

"Of course I am."

"You manage with the girls all right?"

"You needn't worry about that."

"I'm glad. It's easier that way. . . . I'm a selfish bastard. But I shan't change now. Go your own way. When I'm no longer around, I'll soon be forgotten. You can be your own man. I'll look out for what you do."

"Perhaps I'll come over and take a six-month course. Learn some basics from you."

"That'll be the day! See you presently."

"Yeah."

"[illegible] hope I am"
"You manage with the girls all right?"
"You needn't worry about that."
"I'm [illegible]... I'm a selfish bastard, but I shan't change now. Go your own way. When I'm no longer around..."

[From Stephen Luther's diary]

So all three of us were there on that last night. Adrian I saw sitting at the back with some friends. Luke slipped at the last minute into the "house seat" next to mine. As Adrian had prophesied, the report of Matthew's trial had proved good publicity and the theatre was even fuller than usual. Matthew came on to loud applause as ever, but, of course, this audience couldn't tell that he wasn't dressed as he usually was for the opening extract—a scene from one of the Dodie Smith's; he was in evening dress and he advanced right down to the footlights and addressed us. It was a remarkable effort, one of Matthew's very best, combining charm with irony. And if the audience had but known it, they were to get their money's worth, if a performance was what they had come to see.

This is his speech:

"Ladies and Gentlemen. I have to tell you that I am cancelling my performance tonight and terminating this recital. Your money will be refunded to you. I have made all the arrangements and you will be very little delayed as you go out.

"Several theatres in this theatrical avenue begin half an hour later than we do. So it is only the inconvenience that need bother you. You have time to reinvest your seat money more profitably.

"Next door on the right, for instance, you can see a play which re-enacts a ritual murder in the hop-picking country. *The Times* calls it 'an impassioned exploration of the sadistic undertones of modern society'. *The Observer* says of it, 'It goes to the very root of regional violence'. *The Sunday Times* calls it 'a deeply religious experience'.

"If that doesn't appeal to you, next door to the left is a new approach to playwriting where the text has been entirely improvised by the young cast. *The Times* calls it 'a dazzling example of the new techniques which are overhauling our conception of theatre'. *The Observer* calls it 'more natural than naturalism, more real than reality'. *The Sunday Times* calls it 'a deeply religious experience'.

"I have seen both and I can give you my own opinion, for what it is worth. I think they're both CRAP, and why on earth a parcel of only moderately talented actors and actresses should imagine they are also blessed with the divine gift of writing passes my comprehension. But then I'm nearly sixty, which brings me back to the performance which you are not going to see from me tonight.

"For the plain fact is that even crappier than the crap on our left or the crap on our right would have been the crap you would have had to listen to here. Could anything be crappier than taking gobbets and snatches from my past successes and stringing them together as a sort of advertisement for all my mannerisms and affectations? That's the crappy thing. I was inviting you to a joint wallow in nostalgia, and I find it now degrading for both of us. It is an act of prostitution; and I should be asking you to connive in it as *voyeurs*. You are not, I can see, perverts—not all of you, anyhow, and I feel it is my duty to safeguard not only your money but your morals as well. I no longer wish to prostitute myself, and I no longer wish the connivance of an audience in the act of prostitution.

"Those are my last words from the English stage except my humble apologies for inconveniencing you. Thank you. Good night."